The Birdly Wonder is Lost...Again!

I took a step toward her. "Beulah, don't cry. Surely he'll turn up."

She shook her head. "Always before, he's been lucky, but this time...sooner or later, the coyotes will find him." She gazed up at the sky. "I just don't understand why he does this!"

..."Beulah, all I'm saying is that...well, we should try to look at the brighter side."

She stared at me. "The brighter side!"

"Yes ma'am, absolutely. I mean, if he doesn't show up, we'll just have to trudge on without him." I gave her a wink. "And how'd you like to do a little trudging around with me, huh?"

Yipes. Maybe I should have waited to bring up The Brighter Side. I mean, there are times when a guy should shut his beak, right? This seemed to be one of those times. I knew it when her eyes flamed, her nostrils flared, and a torrent of air rushed into her lungs.

And in a tone of voice that would have taken the paint off the side of a barn, she screeched, "Heartless cad! If Plato doesn't come back, there will be no Brighter Side—ever! My last question to you is...*will you help us find him?*"

What! Me?

The Secret Pledge

John R. Erickson

Illustrations by Gerald L. Holmes

Maverick Books, Inc.

MAVERICK BOOKS, INC.
Published by Maverick Books, Inc.
P.O. Box 549, Perryton, TX 79070
Phone: 806.435.7611
www.hankthecowdog.com

First published in the United States of America by Maverick Books, Inc. 2016.

1 3 5 7 9 10 8 6 4 2

LIBRARY OF CONGRESS CONTROL NUMBER: 2016947765

978-1-59188-168-1 (paperback); 978-1-59188-268-8 (hardcover)

Printed in the United States of America

Dedicated to the memory of Joyce Courson, an extraordinary lady and member of our church and community.

CONTENTS

Not a Normal Day on the Ranch

It's me again, Hank the Cowdog. When Drover and I loaded up in Slim Chance's pickup and headed out on our daily feed run, I expected it to be a normal day on the ranch—driving from pasture to pasture, feeding alfalfa hay to several bunches of ungrateful cows, checking windmills, doctoring twelve yearlings in the sick pen, feeding the horses…the usual stuff.

Well, we did the usual stuff, but there was more and we'll get to it in a minute. But first, let's set the scene. It was in the fall, and what a great fall we'd had! Boy, you talk about delicious weather: cool nights and warm, still, golden afternoons without much wind. The flies were pretty bad, but we expect that in the fall. If a fly can't deal out a certain amount misery on a pretty autumn day, he'd have no reason to get out of bed in the morning.

Which brings up an interesting question: Where do the stupid flies go at night? Do they sleep? Do they have beds?

And I'll tell you another interesting question, this one about ants. They live in a dark hole in the ground. They have no lights, not even a candle, and they have no clocks. An ant hole is dark all the time, just as dark at noon as it is at midnight, yet at first light every morning, you see ants creeping around. How do they know when it's time to go to work?

For every interesting question, there's bound to be an equally interesting answer, but on this occasion, I don't have one.

Now, where were we? Oh yes, flies. No, we finished our discussion about flies. We were talking about something more important, but I'm drawing a blank.

You know, this is frustrating. A dog takes pride in commanding a tight ship, making lists, keeping priorities, and tending to the business of running his ranch, then something like this comes along and it takes the window out of his sails. What makes it twice as bad is that sails don't even have windows, and at some point, you begin to wonder…

Phooey. I'm sorry, I seem to be…wait. We were feeding cattle on the first day of November and met a very important Someone on the county road. Who? Be patient, we're getting there.

As I recall, we had loaded twenty bales of alfalfa hay in the back of the pickup. Actually, in the interest of fairness and honesty, I'll admit that Slim had loaded the hay, but I had taken on the huge responsibility of supervising his work, which meant that every time he lifted a bale, I was standing by to pounce upon whatever form of vermin might be living beneath the bales.

We're talking about mice and field rats. They seem to think the hay stack belongs to *them*. Without anybody's permission, they build subway tunnels and mouse-towns down there, and it's my job to set 'em straight on who owns the hay stacks on this outfit. ME.

We have regulations. No building permit? Fine. No tunnel, no town, no mouse nests, and no secret stashes of turkey corn. (They steal some of the corn Sally May puts out for the wild turkeys). Every winter, I have to clear 'em out and send 'em packing. They never go far, of course, but sooner or later, they run out of hay bales under which to

build and burrow, because we feed all the hay. At that point, I don't know where they go, but they become somebody else's problem.

Anyway, we got the hay loaded and were on our way to feed the east side of the ranch. We were on the county road and a pickup approached us from the east. Slim recognized the vehicle, stopped in the middle of the road, and started gabbing with Billy, one of the neighboring ranchers.

For a while I listened as they covered the usual topics: the grass, the weather, quail season, cattle prices, and whatever the almanac was predicting for the winter. I confess that my attention began to wander and I was finding it hard to stay awake.

But then Drover poked me in the ribs and gasped, "Oh my gosh, it's...it's Miss Beulah!"

Oh mercy me! You talk about something that will bring me roaring out of a nap! My eyes snapped open and I caught a glimpse of her, sitting in the back of Billy's pickup—Miss Beulah the Collie, the girl of my dreams, the most gorgeous collie gal in Texas.

When I saw her, my eyes bugged out and my heart went into a spell of pittypatapations. Sorry, that's a big word, so let's break it down. Pittypat-a-pations. It's a medical term, don't you see, and it means that your heart starts jumping around in your chest like a couple of jackrabbits in a sack.

Yes, by George, the very mention of her name caused my heart to jump around. You know, I didn't want to make a scene or cause any trouble, but Slim happened to be sitting between me and the open window, and...well, things happened. On my way out the window, I might have left some claw marks on his arm, tore a button off his shirt, and knocked his hat down on his nose.

"Hank, for crying out loud!"

To be honest, I hardly noticed, because my mind had already shifted into a Higher Dimension of Reality. See, for years I had been trying to win her heart and capture the torch of her love, and we're talking about using every trek in the beak, but somehow nothing had worked. Trick in the book.

It was baffling, maddening, discouraging, and frustrating, and you can multiply all those words by ten, because...sorry, I don't mean to get all worked up, but this had been a matter of deepest concern. See, not only had she resisted my charms, but she seemed to have some kind of weird affection for a bird dog.

A BIRD DOG!

Getting trounced in the Arena of Love would have been bad enough in itself, but getting trounced by a skinny, stick-tailed, pea-brained bird-merchant was almost more than I could bear. And, in case you haven't figured it out yet, we're talking about Plato.

I'm sure you remember Plato, a spotted bird dog with about as much sense as fishing bait. He and Beulah lived on the same ranch, and where you saw one, you usually saw the other. They went places together. They were friends.

Actually, they were more than friends, and that was the crutch of the crust of my problem. I won't say that it made me jealous. Everyone knows that jealousy is a petty emotion, so let's just say that I was...no, by George, let's go ahead and dive right into the truth.

I was jealous. There. It's out in the open for all the world to see.

How could she care about such a goofball? It was beyond reason...and, actually, therein lay my only hope. See, Beulah's affection for the dumbbell was so crazy and out of character, I clanged to the belief that I was only one step away from Sweet and Ultimate Victory.

Some days, that's all that got me out of bed

and kept me going, no kidding, the flick flimmer... the flim flicker...the faint flicker of hope, there we go, that one day, her eyes would open and she would come to her senses.

One trick, that's all I needed—one song, one blast of romantic poetry, one drop of a magic love potion behind my ears—and she would be MINE.

So there you are, a glimpse into the secret dungeon of my heart. It helps to explain why I stampeded across Slim's lap and dived out the window, and why I didn't give a rip if I had torn his shirt.

A little humor there to lighten the atmosphere. Did you get it? See, I didn't give a *rip* about *tearing* his shirt. Ha ha. Rip and tear. Ha ha. You know, humor is very important to the over-all so-forth, and we must never get so swept up in our sorrows that can't pause to....

Never mind. I had caught a glimpse of Miss Beulah and it appeared that this might be my Big Chance. Was it, really? To find out, you'll have to keep reading.

A Bad Start

I clawed my way over Slim and dived out the window, hit the ground and sprinted around to the back of Billy's pickup. There, I drew myself up into a Pose of Dignity, took a wide stance, and gazed up into the face of my...

I gazed up into the face of Plato the Bird Dog, my second-worst enemy in the world (after the cat). He stood at the back of the pickup, looking down at me with that big, happy bird dog grin on his face—the one where his long sloppy tongue hangs out one side of his mouth.

"Hank! By golly, great to see you again. Hey, first day of bird season, what do you think, huh? Great, you bet. You know, Hank, I've been on a new training program this year and I think I'm coming out of the pre-season in the best shape of my life. Pecs and abs, Hank, that's where it starts, and I've been building up the bottoms of my feet, too."

"I'd like to speak to Beulah."

"Those feet are so important, Hank, so important. The thing is, you forget how much cactus we have in these pastures, and if you don't get your feet toughed up, by golly, two hours in the field and you're done. How about your feet, Hank, how are they holding up?"

"They take me where I want to go."

He laughed. "Good line, I like that. 'They take me where I want to go.' Ha ha. But, seriously, Hank, we all get so busy, we overlook the..."

"I'd like to speak with Beulah."

"Beulah? Oh. Great. She's here." He turned toward the front. "Honey Bunch? Guess who's here. Old Hank, by golly." He turned back to me and gave me a wink. "She'll be right with you. She's fixing her ears."

"What's wrong with her ears?"

"Well, she's...you know how she is, Hank, every hair in place, always looking like a million dollars. Isn't she something? Whoa, hang on, Bud, here she comes!"

The nitwit stepped aside and...gasp...there

she was in all her glory and splinter. The pittypatapations in my heart struck again, and we're talking about a heart that was banging like a bass drum. I tried to speak but the words seemed frozen in my mouse.

In my mouth, that is. I had already taken care of the mouses. The meese. The mooses. Skip it.

She had fixed her ears, all right, and her nose and her eyes and every single hair, and the total effect left me speechless, so I stared. I gawked. She gave me a smile. "Hello, Hank. You're looking well."

It took me a moment to unthaw my speech mechanisms. "Thank you, ma'am, but looks don't always tell the story."

"Oh? Have you been ill?"

You know, I had walked into this situation, thinking that I would pursue a Go Slow Program—recite a poem, sing a song, talk about flowers or something—but now that she was right in front of me, I tossed caution out the window and went plunging toward the bottom line.

"Of course I've been ill! Since I saw you last, I haven't been able to eat or sleep. I walk around at night like a ghost. I've lost twenty pounds. My hair is falling out. I'm losing teeth. Even the fleas are moving out."

Her mouth fell open. "Oh Hank, that's terrible! What seems to be the problem? Do you have a disease?"

"No, Beulah, *you* have a disease." I stabbed a paw in the air toward the bird dog. "HIM. He's worse than mange. He's worse than cholera. How can I lead a normal, healthy life when you're wasting your time with him?"

Plato had been listening, of course, and thought it was time to open his big yap. "Hank, if I may intrude here, you've raised several points that we should..."

"Dry up." Back to Beulah. "There's a simple solution, right before your eyes."

"Hank, please..."

"I'm the solution. Me, the cowdog of your dreams."

"It's not that simple."

"Of course it is. Ditch him, get rid of him, send him down the road!"

"Are you finished?"

"No ma'am, I'm just getting warmed up."

"Well, you'll have to excuse me, I have things to do. Maybe we can talk about it another time."

I couldn't believe it. She stuck her snooty nose in the air, and left me and the Quail King alone in a poisonous silence. Plato shrugged and grinned. "Well! Perfect weather for a hunt, Hank, and they say the quail numbers are up this year."

I roasted him with a glare. He didn't notice and went right on blabbering.

"You know, Hank, and when bird season's over, by golly, we ought to sit down and, you know, have a real heart-to-heart talk, just me and you. Guy-talk." At that moment, Billy started his pickup and pulled away. Plato waved a paw. "Well, here we go, Hank, opening day! Great to see you again! I hope you get to feeling better."

Oh yeah? Well, we didn't need to talk about what I hoped for him.

As the pickup sped off to the west, I studied the lonely figure sitting near the cab. Was she weeping? Looking back at me through tear-drenched eyes?

No. Bummer.

I made my way back to the pickup, knowing that I would have to listen to Slim gripe and complain. Sure enough, that's what he did. He rolled up his shirt sleeve and pointed to several red scratch marks on his arm, then pointed to the place on his shirt where, once upon a time, a little button had lived.

"Bozo. You liked to have tore my clothes off.

How am I going to get that button sewed back on my shirt? I don't even own a needle and thread."

This might have gone on for hours, but, lucky for me, an oil field tanker truck had pulled up behind us and blew his air horn. Slim almost jumped out of his skin, but what did he expect? We'd been parked in the middle of the county road for twenty minutes, but guess who got blamed. Me.

"Bozo."

Fine. I made my way across the seat and shoved Drover out of the Shotgun Position. After a moment of silence, he said, "How'd it go with Beulah?"

"Not so great."

"I'll be derned. What did you tell her?"

"Is that any of your business?"

"Just curious."

"Well, if you must know, I told her to ditch Plato."

"Just like that?"

"Yes, just like that. I went straight to the point."

"Maybe that was the wrong approach."

I barbecued him with a glare. "What do you know about approaches to women?"

"Well, I know that yours flopped."

That hurt. I heaved a heavy sigh and turned my gaze out the window. "In small but tiny ways, you have a point. Maybe I was too blunt."

"You were too blunt. She's not a bulldozer."

"Drover, she's a lady, not a bulldozer. Here's a thought. Next time, I'll try to be more subtle." I turned back to the runt. "Why are your eyes crossed?"

"Oh, I was about to sneeze."

"So sneeze."

"Well, it passed."

"Good, but please don't cross you eyes when I'm trying to give you lessons on romance. It makes me think you're not paying attention."

"Sorry."

"One of these days, when you grow up, if you ever grow up, you might need some tips on charming the ladies.

"Yeah, I think she likes me."

"But I can't help you if you're crossing your eyes all the time."

"She loves my poetry."

"The point to remember is that we don't approach the ladies as though they were heavy equipment. Technique is very important."

"Got it, thanks."

Whew. Some dogs require more tutoring than others, and Drover requires a lot. I mean, he wears me out. I try to be patient with the little mutt. I want to pass along helpful tips from my Archive of

Wisdom, but let's be honest: It's very hard to help a dog who spends half his life sneezing and crossing his eyes.

Oh well. Life moves on and so does a ranch pickup on a feeding day. We had work to do and we did it, even though my heart had been badly damaged. I could only hope that fate would allow me one more chance to woo back the Lady of My Dreams.

The next morning brought us bright sunlight that glistened on frost-covered trees and grass. By the time I had finished Morning Patrol, the frost had melted away and the day had turned out warm and beautiful, with the temperature nudging up into the fifties. We're talking about gorgeous, perfect autumn weather.

To be honest, the day was so pleasant, I found it hard to concentrate on my daily workload of work. I mean, in the wintertime, sometimes it's too cold for me to get excited about work, and sometimes in the summer, it's too hot. In the fall of the year...well, by George, once in a while on a delicious fall afternoon, it's just too nice for work, and sometimes a guy yields to the temptation to...

Maybe we shouldn't be talking about this. You know how I am about the children. I wouldn't want them to get the wrong idea, that I'm a lazy bum who takes naps in the afternoon.

That's the kind of behavior we expect from Drover, but me? Hey, I'm Head of Ranch Security, not a lazy bum, so it's very unlikely that you'll ever find me napping on a warm autumn day. No sir. I might be lying in a warm patch of sun, but I'll be hard at work, running spreadsheets or reading reports or updating my logbook of Drover's Chicken Marks.

You talk about hard work! Keeping a record of Drover's Chicken Marks is a full-time job. It would wear out five ordinary mutts, but I have to do it all myself, in my so-called spare time.

Have you ever seen that book? You talk about HUGE. Two thousand pages, thirty-four pounds of Chicken Marks. Sometimes, when Drover has a good day, we delete a few, but most of the time, we're adding them.

We keep that logbook in our vault in the Security Division's Vast Office Complex. It's open for public inspection every Thursday between two and one o'clock in the aftermath. If you're ever in the neighborhood, you should drop by and read it. It will give you a shocking glimpse at exactly what the King of Slackers has been doing all these years.

But the whole point of this discussion is that

after spending hours and hours, bringing the logbook up to date, I was exhausted, just flat worn out and, well, on warm autumn days, occasionally a guy's eyelids begin to droop.

Sometimes my eyelids seem to have a mind of their own, don't you see. On this occasion, school was out, so to speak, and the eyelids were running the show. They staged a mutiny and began drifting in a downward direction, and before I knew it...well, perhaps I dozed, but it had nothing to do with my being a lazy bum.

Yes, I dozed, and even better, I fell into the embrace of a delicious dream about...can you guess who? Stand by, we're fixing to watch a dream.

LOADING DREAM SEQUENCE #357-753

Loading...loading...loafing...loading

Enter Password

****

Re-enter Dream Sequence Password!

You forgot your password, didn't you?

Dummy

Stand by...

Dream Sequence #357-753 is ready!

Dream Sequence #357-753

Mercy! There I stood, outside the castle, gazing up into the face of the lovely, incomparable Miss Beulah the Collie. Her father, the wicked king, had locked her in the tower, don't you see, and she was looking down at me with pleading eyes.

A glance at the cold, gray blocks of stone told me that I could never scale the walls and save her, so in my most muniferous voice, I called out…

ME: "Miss Beulah, Miss Beulah, let down your long hair!"

BEULAH: "Oh Hankie, oh Hankie, I have none to spare."

ME: "I'm sure that you do, two braids, gold

and long."

BEULAH: "My hair is too short, I fear you are wrong."

ME: "Oh, Beulah, Miss Beulah, then lower a cable."

BEULAH: "Oh, Hankie, I can't. It's tied to the table."

ME: "Then quickly, my love, let down a long rope."

BEULAH: "You'd better wake up, Hank, you sound like a dope."

WHAT?

Did you hear that last line? Something was wrong, and I mean seriously wrong. In the first place, Miss Beulah would never suggest that I sounded like "a dope," and in the second place, she would never have told me to wake up when I wasn't asleep.

Wait. Could this have all been part of a... maybe I was asleep and dreaming the whole episode. Yes, of course. Hang on a second.

DREAM SEQUENCE IS CLOSING DOWN

I rushed to the intercom and issued a command. "Open eyelids one and two! Surface, surface!"

We went zooming up from the depths and my eyelids drifted into the Open Position. I found myself looking at…well, some dog with a silly grin on his mouth. I glanced around. "Who are you?"

"I'm Drover. Hi."

"Hi. What happened to the castle?"

"Well, I don't know, but I think you were asleep."

"I was NOT asleep." I blinked my eyes and glanced around. "Wait, maybe I did drift off, and you're Drover, right?"

"Yep, it's me, same old Drover. Hi."

"We've already said 'hi.'"

"Sorry."

"You're welcome."

"Thanks. I guess you were dreaming about Beulah."

I paced a few steps away and tried to clear the fog out of my bog. "Maybe that was it, but it was so real! She was locked in the castle and I heard her voice, just as though she had been as close as you and me."

He grinned. "Well, she was…sort of."

"She was here? Tell me, I must know! She was here, in the flesh?"

"Well, not in the flesh."

"Good grief, what was she in?"

"Well, she was me. I said her lines."

"What?" I thundered over to him. "You trespassed on my dream and said Beulah's lines without permission?"

"Yep, and it was fun too. I just love making rhymes."

"Oh yeah? Well, here's a rhyme: Ten Chicken Marks! This will go into the logbook."

"Yeah, but it's not a rhyme."

"Okay, twenty Chicken Marks."

"Gosh, how come it went up?"

"It went up because..." I paced away from the little lunatic and took a deep breath of air. "This is very confusing, but I'm beginning to see a pattern. I was exhausted and fell asleep."

"I knew you were asleep."

"Please don't argue with me. I drifted into a light doze and was dreaming about Miss Beulah, but here's the impointant poink."

"What's a poink?"

"The poink is that you had no right to invade my dream and spout lines of poetry, pretending that you were Miss Beulah."

"Sorry."

"Are you really sorry or just saying it?"

"Just saying it. It was fun."

"Just as I suspected. Thirty Chicken Marks!"

"What if I told you a secret?"

"It wouldn't change a thing. Bribery is not..." I marched back over to him. "What secret?"

"Well, if I told you, it wouldn't be a secret."

"Don't get smart with me, pal. Out with it."

"Will you trade my secret for some Chicken Marks?"

"How many are we talking about?"

"Oh, a hundred?"

"Out of the question, no way."

"Thirty?"

"Okay, thirty. And this had better be good."

"It is, you'll love it."

You're probably aching and quivering to hear the secret, but...I hate to tell you this. It's just too secret to tell. No kidding. It's Highly, Widely and Deeply Classified. There's no way you'll ever be able to...oh, maybe it won't hurt to reveal it.

Okay, Drover and I had negotiated a deal. He agreed to tell me a Big Secret if I removed thirty Chicken Marks from his logbook, which we keep under lock and key in the...we've already covered that.

The runt was so excited about his secret, he could hardly sit still. "Are you ready for this? Hang on, it's a good one."

"Please hurry up. I have a busy schedule this afternoon."

"Yeah, I noticed."

"I beg your pardon?"

"I said, here we go." Grinning like an I-don't-know-what, he leaned toward me and...I couldn't believe this part...he lost his balance, fell into me, and caused me to tumble over backwards.

I leaped to my feet. "Will you stop goofing off and get to the point?"

"Sorry. This secret's got me so excited, I can hardly talk."

"Well, talk anyway. This is costing me thirty Chicken Marks. And don't bump into me again."

"Okay, I'll try." He glanced over both shoulders and lowered his voice. "You dreamed that you were talking to Miss Beulah, right?"

"That's correct, only I had no idea that you were saying her lines. Do you have any idea how that makes me feel?"

"Do you want to hear this or not?"

"Please try to keep a respectful tongue in your head. You're speaking to the Head of Ranch Security."

He inched closer. "What would you say if I told you that she's here?"

"Who's here?"

"Miss Beulah."

"On this ranch? Right now?"

"Yep, honest, no fooling."

I glanced around in a full circle and saw no one. "I'd say, number one, that she isn't here, which means, number two, that you're wrong. And number three, I'd say that you're either having hallucitanias or telling a whopperous lie. Drover, this story will never sell."

"Bet me?"

"I beg your pardon?"

"Let's bet on it."

"I...I never make wagers during office hours."

He'd caught me off guard, don't you see. What was going on here? Again, I glanced around in a full circle and saw no sign of anyone. Even more crucible, I hadn't heard the sound of a vehicle coming into headquarters. Do you see the meaning of this important clue? If Beulah had come to the ranch, she would have been riding in the back of Billy's pickup—and I would have heard it.

Oh, I know what you're thinking. I was asleep and wouldn't have heard a vehicle coming into headquarters. Isn't that what you were thinking?

Ha. Let me clear up that little misunderstanding. See, my ears are very sensitive listening devices. On the Microwave Frequency, they can pick up the tiniest of sounds, and we're talking about a mouse taking ballet lessons in the next county.

See, my ears NEVER SLEEP. There. Is that impressive or what?

These thoughts and clues were flying around inside my head, and they were all pointing in the same direction. Bottom Line: Drover had offered to make a wild, foolish wager. Would I take advantage of the little mutt and accept his bet?

Yes, but I would be doing it for a higher purpose. He needed to be taught a lesson about gambling on the job.

I turned back to him. "I never make bets during business hours, but this time, I'm going to make an exception. State your bet."

He was practically drooling with excitement. "Oh goodie. I'll bet that Beulah's on the ranch, right now."

"And we're talking about the real, actual, flesh-and-blood Beulah, not some filament of your imagination?"

"Yep."

"And not your voice, pretending to be Beulah?"

"Yep."

He was really digging himself a hole on this one. "What are we betting? And let me be up-front. I'm not interested in playing penny-ante, toothpick-poker with you. Whomsoever loses this deal should feel some pain."

He rolled his eyes around and appeared to be giving it heavy thought. "Let's see here. Whomsoever loses has to sing 'Happy Birthday' to the cat."

"What a weird bet."

"Yeah, but will you take it?"

I didn't want to tip my hand, but I couldn't hold bark a back of laughter...hold back a bark of laughter, let us say. "Ha ha ha. Yes, I'll take it, and I hope you can remember the words to the Birthday Song."

"Oh, I'll manage. Shake on it?"

We didn't actually shake paws. We bumped paws. This was a new and kind of high-fashion way of doing things. City dogs all over Texas were doing it that way and, well, I try to stay on top of the latest trends and fashions.

So we bumped paws and sealed the deal. Poor Drover! He had really stepped in a trap this time, and the sad part was that he had built it himself. Oh well. You can't spend your whole life trying to protect a dunce from his own duncery.

He was still wearing that crazy grin. "Let's run up to the machine shed and see if we can find Miss Beulah."

"Here's a better idea. Let's *walk* up to the machine shed. You'll get your medicine soon enough." We started up the hill in a nice slow walk. "You know, singing 'Happy Birthday' to the cat is really going to hurt. To be honest, I can't think of any kind of torture that would be worse."

"Yeah, it'll be awful, 'cause Pete's going to love it."

"Exactly my point. He's such an unbearable little sneak…look, Drover, I enjoy winning as much as any dog, but this might be too much. If you want to back out of the deal, we can work out some kind of settlement. We can move those thirty Chicken Marks back into your account and cancel the bet. What do you say?"

"Oh, I'll stick with the bet. We shook on it."

"Okay, pal, have it your way. Don't say that I didn't try to help you."

"Yeah, you've been a great help."

Poor little Drover. What is the Wise Old Saying? "None is so blind as him who won't turn up his hearing aid?"

No, that's not it. "None is so blind as him who won't open the blinds?"

Still not it. "None is so blind as him who…"

Tell you what, we'll come back to the Wise Old Sayings another time. The one I had in mind really captured this situation, but I can't remember it. Sorry, it was a good one. For now, we'll have to settle for another Wise Old Saying: "PHOOEY."

I thought that was pretty clever, using "phooey" as a Wise Old Saying. Ha ha. Did you get it? See, "phooey" is a word we use when our mind has drawn a blank and...maybe you got it, so let's move along to the good part.

Mister Smarty Pants was about to step in his own trap.

This Really Hurts

Okay, here we go. Drover was about to step into his own trap, and while I couldn't help feeling a certain wicked satisfaction that the Cause of Justice was about to be served, I also couldn't help feeling a little sting of...well, sadness, I suppose.

Yes, sadness or regret. It's the feeling a parent feels when he has to watch, helpless, as his child does something really dumb and then has to suffer the consequences.

As mature adults, we understand that true education often comes from bitter experience. We understand that it's a natural part of the learning process. We understand all of that, yet we can't help feeling some compassion as the Hammer of

Knowledge comes down on the head of a poor, misguided friend.

I mean, can you imagine anything *worse* than having to sing "Happy Birthday" to a sneaking, sniveling, arrogant little crook of a cat? I couldn't. If I sang a song to the little creep—we're talking about Pete, of course, Mister Never Sweat—it would be...well, we needn't go into all the dark details. Fortunately, it was a fate I would never have to experience.

Anyway, there was a certain air of sadness in the sad air as we made our sad walk up the sad hill to the machine shed. Casting glances to my right, I could see that my assistant was still wearing that clown's face, with a huge painted grin that stretched from ear to shining sea.

Sea? Now I remember the Wise Old Saying. "None is so blind as him who will not *see*." There we go. I get a kick out of using Wise Old Sayings, and this one underscored the point that Drover had no idea what lay in his future.

By the time we reached the top of the hill, he was huffing and puffing, because...well, let's be honest. He doesn't get the proper amount of daily exercise. He never does anything. He sits around all day, snapping at flies or staring at the clouds. Hencely, by the time we arrived at the machine shed, he was out of breath.

Me? I hardly noticed the climb up the hill, and there was no mystery about it: diet, exercise, discipline. On an average day, I have to make at least one patrol of ranch headquarters, don't you know, which requires that I…

Huh?

Someone was standing in front of the machine shed, in fact, several someones. I recognized one of them right away. Did you notice the tall guy on the left? Well, you weren't there, so never mind. I recognized the tall, skinny guy on the left. Slim Chance. I knew him very well.

But there was another man standing beside him, not as tall as Slim and thicker in the shoulders. Like Slim, he dressed cowboy—faded jeans, wide leather belt, blue denim shirt with snap buttons, felt hat with sweat stains around the crown. At first glance, I didn't recognize him.

But here's the part that will blow you away. Sitting at the feet of the cowboy-stranger was… hang on to something solid…sitting at the feet of the stranger was a COLLIE DOG, and we're not talking about just any old, ordinary Raggedy Ann collie dog. We're talking about the most gorgeous collie gal I'd ever laid eyes on.

And speaking of eyes, mine almost bugged out

of my head. My thoughts tumbled like autumn leaves in a whirlwind, and for a moment I feared I might faint. Unless my eyes had decided to play a trick on me, I was looking at Billy, the same guy who'd stopped on the county road only yesterday, and his dog, MISS BEULAH THE COLLIE!

Beside me, I heard Drover's voice. Would you like to guess what he said? You'll never guess, so I'll tell you, and this is an exact quote. He said, "Hee hee hee!"

My mind swirled and my eyes darted back and forth. At last I was able to speak. "Drover, remember what I said about not betting during business hours? I've been thinking about that. Our wager went against regulations."

"Yeah, but we already made the bet."

"Exactly my point. We made a bet that was illegal, immoral, and against Regulations. We did it in haste, in a careless moment. I'm sure that's bothering you."

"Nope, not a bit."

"Of course it is. You're a law-abiding little doggie, and I've always admired that, so you'll be thrilled to know that there might be a way we can get out of this awkward situation." He stared at me. "You are thrilled, aren't you?"

"Not yet."

"Of course not, because we haven't gotten to the thrilling part. Listen to this." I began pacing back and forth in front of him, as I often do when I'm trying to unfurl a huge concept. "Drover, you'll be thrilled to know there's a tiny, obscure clause in the Cowdog Handbook, stating that careless bets can be reversed with something called 'an Unbet.'"

"Unbet?"

"Exactly, so you've heard it? Great. See, all we have to do is issue an Unbet and it wipes out the pointless, illegal wager we made in a careless moment. It takes us back to Square One."

He rolled his eyes up to the clouds. "Yeah, but I kind of like Square Two."

I fought to control my temper. "All right, forget Square One. If your mother was here today, standing in front of you and looking into your eyes, what would she say?"

"Well, the last time I saw her, she told me to get a job. Oh, and she told me not to scratch in public."

"Scratch in...Drover, if your mother was here, she would he horrified that you made a crooked bet."

"Yeah, but it wasn't crooked."

"Of course it was crooked! Somehow you

knew that Miss Beulah was here on the ranch, but you didn't inform me."

"Yeah, it would have ruined the bet."

"Don't get smart with me, soldier. Maybe you'd better tell this court how you knew about this. I didn't hear a pickup coming into headquarters. Do you see any sign of Billy's pickup?"

"Nope."

"So do you expect this court to believe that Billy and his dog *walked* into headquarters? Is that the story you're telling under oath?"

He grinned. "Yep. I saw 'em coming."

"You...this is an outrage! You saw a man and his dog walking into headquarters and didn't inform the Head of Ranch Security?"

"Well, I tried but you were asleep."

"Objection. Five Chicken Marks!"

"And you never listen anyway."

"Ten Chicken Marks!"

I was cooked. Somehow I had blundered right into the middle of a trap that Drover was supposed to have set for himself. I couldn't believe it. I took a deep breath and paced a few steps away.

"All right, Drover, we've reached The Bottom Line, the point in a discussion where we ask, 'What do you really hope to achieve with your life?' I want you to give that careful thought. I mean, this is very important."

He wadded up his face in a pose of deep concentration. That was a good sign. Maybe his better nature was beginning to stir. I waited and at last he spoke. "What I really want to achieve with my life is...to hear you sing 'Happy Birthday' to the cat. Hee hee."

My eyes bulged and I roared, "Weasel! I can't believe you'd..." I struggled to regain my composure and marched back to him. "Here's an idea. You'll like this. Let's...let's postpone the hanging....the, uh, singing for a couple of weeks. I'll need time to rehearse." He shook his head. "I agree, so let's schedule it for next week." He shook his head. "Day-after-tomorrow?" He shook his head. "Okay, you little cheater, when?"

"Oh, let's do it now."

"Now! You expect me to..."

Oh brother. I was cooked beyond all previous cookings. Have you ever wondered how it would feel to make the long march to your own hanging? I can tell you: terrible. Every step took me closer to a fate so awful, I could hardly bear to think about it.

Good grief, I had to sing "Happy Birthday" to my worst enemy in the whole world!

You're probably wondering what kept me going, how I was able to mustard the mayonnaise to go through with it. Well, a deep sense of honor was a big part of it. As you know, cowdogs are just a little bit special. We're made from better stuff than ordinary mutts. We always tell the truth and we always pay off our gambling debts, no matter how badly it hurts.

Holding my head high, I marched down to the yard gate, accompanied by the little cheater who had set me up and lured me into this mess. When we arrived at the gate, the cat was nowhere in sight, so I said, "He's not here. We'll try it another time."

"Oh, I'll call him. Hey, Pete? Pete? Yoo-hoo, we've got a surprise for you."

It was my rotten luck that Kitty was lurking in the iris patch, where he always lurks, and heard Drover's voice. Most of the time, when you call a cat, he takes off in the opposite direction. I mean, they're highly trained to do the exact opposite of what anyone wants them to do.

But this time, Kitty must have sensed that something was afoot. His scheming little face appeared out of the flowers, and here he came, sliding and slithering and rubbing his way down the fence. When he reached the gate, he studied

us with his cunning little eyes and spoke in his usual, annoying tone of voice.

"Well, well! It's Hankie the Wonderdog and his comical sidekick! To what do we owe this unexpected visit?"

My whole body trembled with righteous anger, and I could feel my twips lipping into a snarl. Drover, on the other hand, seemed almost beside himself with cheating glee.

"Hi, Pete. Boy, this is going to be fun."

"Oh really. Tell me about the fun. I can hardly wait."

"Well, Hank and I made a bet, see, and he lost. I couldn't believe he went for it. Hee hee. And now he has to sing 'Happy Birthday'...to you!"

Would I be able to go through with this outrage? You'll never know unless you keep reading.

This Hurts Even Worse

I hate this, but let's get it over with.

Kitty's eyes moved from me to Drover, and he began flicking the last inch of his creepy little snake of a tail. "Sing to me? Little old kitty me? Well, my goodness! It's not exactly my birthday, but..." He sputtered a laugh. "...well, who could pass up an opportunity like this? I guess we'll have to shuffle the calendar and say that it's my..." He snickered again. "...my birthday. And, yes, it does sound like fun."

Have you ever heard the term "doorknob volcano"? A doorknob volcano appears to be just an ordinary, innocent, quiet mountain. It might even be covered with pine trees and snow. It makes the kind of pretty picture that you might put on the front of a Christmas card.

But it has a secret. Deep inside, the doorknob volcano burns with a raging fire, hot enough to melt rocks and turn them into a river of hissing lava. And nobody suspects a thing until the top blows off the mountain.

That was ME.

But we need to pause here to make a little correction. We said that volcanoes come in two varieties: the kind the blows up and the kind that just sits there, wearing trees and snow and looking innocent. Our vocabulary word for that session was "doorknob" and it described the second variety, the one that just sits there—the doorknob volcano.

Well, we've found a little problem. The word is supposed to be "dormant" instead of "doorknob." There is no such thing as a doorknob volcano. In fact, it sounds ridiculous. A volcano that sits there, looking innocent but seething inside, is a *dormant* volcano, DOR-MANT, and it has nothing to do with doors or doorknobs. Volcanoes don't have doors.

Sorry for the confusion. We're not sure what went wrong. All I can say is that managing a cattle ranch is a huge responsibility and, well, mistakes happen. Also, I can reveal that we're running diagnostics at this very moment. If this was a conspiracy, we will catch the villains.

Do we have suspects? Yes. You might have picked up on the fact that this glitch hit our systems at the very moment I was standing in front of the cat, when I was trembling with rage because I had been snookered into singing "Happy Birthday" to the little pestilence.

Was there a connection? Was Pete behind this mysterious glitch that had messed up our discussion of volcanoes? Is it a mere coincidence that these things always seem to happen when the cat shows up? At this point, we have no solid proof, but it looks very fishy to me.

Anyway, we're on the case. If Pete has been sabotaging our vocabulary lessons, we WILL get to the bottom of it and he WILL get parked in the nearest tree.

Sorry, I didn't mean to get carried away, but you know how I am about the kids. Cats don't care if the kids go around talking gibberish like a bunch of baboons, eating bananas and dropping the peelings on the ground, picking fleas off their ears and using incorrect vocabulary words. Dogs CARE. Cats don't give a hoot.

Well, let's settle down, take a deep breath, and move along.

Where were we? Oh yes, baboons. One of the

things that makes baboons especially interesting to dogs is that...well, we have human friends who remind us so much...

Never mind the baboons. My so-called friend, Drover C. Dog, had tricked me into making a bonehead wager, and I was about to pay off my debt by....

This is almost too much. I'm not sure I can go on with it. Would you be upset if we just, well, skipped this part? I mean, Life has its dark moments, I don't deny that, but it has brighter moments too, and we shouldn't dwell on the dark and ugly parts, right?

See, we could leave out the song and skip to the part with Miss Beulah. Don't forget that she was on our ranch at the very moment all this nonsense was happening at the yard gate, and who wants to talk about the cat when the most gorgeous dog in all of Texas is up at the machine shed?

Not me. What do you think?

Groan.

Okay, let's get it over with.

We were at the yard gate—me, the cat, and a little traitor named Drover C. Dog. Under the Betting Laws of the State of Texas, I was required to sing "Happy Birthday" to the cat. I couldn't get out of it and I was seething inside like a doorknob volcano.

Kitty was waiting—gleeful, eyes shining, an insolent smirk flashing on his mouth like a neolon sign. A nylon sign. A neon sign, let us say, flashing with such gaudy colors, it made me ill just to look at the little creep.

He fluttered his eyelids and widened his smirk. "Well? Should I hum the opening pitch?"

"I'll handle the opening pitch, you little snipe, and it's liable to be a fast ball—high and inside."

He smirked. "Oh, I get it. You went from a singing pitch to a baseball pitch. How clever! But the song, Hankie, are we going to hear the song?" He gave me a wink. "It's my birthday, you know."

Boy, this was tough, but I must let you in on a secret. See, a wicked plan had begun to glimmer in the dark caverns of my mind, and we're talking about the part of a dog's mind where bats fly around and every sound makes an echo. I would sing the song, but I would seed it with some hidden messages. Here, listen to this.

> Happy birthday to you. (Not!)
> Happy birthday to you. (Not, not!)
> Happy birthday, you reptile.
> Happy birthday to you. NOT!

Heh heh. Was that wicked or what? I had discharged my duty but I had also...the cat was shaking his head. "Won't work, Hankie."

"What do you mean, won't work? I sang the song. I'm out of here."

"Not so fast." He slid his cunning gaze to Drover. "Don't you think he should be required to sing it *nice*?"

Drover looked confused. "Well, I didn't think of that."

"It seemed to lack...well, sincerity. After all, it's my birthday and I want my song to be nice and sincere. I'm sure you'll agree."

Drover studied on that. "Well, it did seem a little snotty."

"Very snotty."

Drover nodded. "Yeah, it seemed very snotty and maybe he could do it again, nicer this time. And I'll sing with him."

The cat clapped his paws together. "What a wonderful idea!" His gaze slithered back to me. "Maybe you could try it again, Hankie, but this time, make it sweeter and more sincere."

I could hardly contain the volcanic pressure that was building up behind my eyeballs. "All right, you little viper, I'll do it again. You want sweet, I'll give you sweet. I hope it gives you sugar diabetes."

And with that, I did a sweetened version of the birthday song—anything to get it over with and move on with my life. You might want to cover your ears. Not only was it a pathetic song, but Drover sang harmony.

Happy birthday to you.
(Sugar crystals all around)
Happy birthday to you.
(Thick molasses dripping down)
Happy birthday, dear Petie.
(I'm sincere, I'm so sincere!)
Happy birthday to you.
(Nice and sweet)

Oh barf. Oh gag. I could hardly believe that I had been involved in producing such a piece of musical trash, but there it was.

The cat clapped his paws together in a silly charade of applause. "That was better, Hankie, but...well, I don't mean to criticize, but the second version still seemed to lack..." He fluttered his eyelashes. "...warmth and honesty. Maybe you could do it one more time."

I stormed over to the fence and glared at him through the wire. "Maybe I could but maybe I

won't. That's all you get. I did my duty and my gambling debts are paid. Here's wishing you mange and indigestion." I beamed a glare at Drover. "Traitor! This will all come out at your court martial."

And with that, I whirled around, raised my head to a proud angle, and marched away, leaving them to whisper and giggle and enjoy their little moment of triumph.

Behind me, I heard Drover say, "Gosh, what's wrong with him? I thought it was a pretty neat song."

"Oh, don't worry. Some dogs are just sore losers. Drover, I thought your harmony part was...well, sublime. It almost brought tears to my eyes."

"No fooling? Hee hee. I didn't know I was such a good singer."

"Oh, you are, you are! One of these days, you should go on tour."

Did you hear that? What a pack of lies! Drover's singing was sub-lime, all right, even lower than the taste of bitter fruit—a little humor there, at a time when there wasn't much else to laugh about. Did you get it? Sub-lime. Lower than...maybe it wasn't all that great.

The point is that I had discharged my duty

and it was time for me to get back to more important things, such as…well, trying to salvage what was left of my love life. I had made a mess of it the day before, but here's a clue you might have missed.

Before the Happy Birthday Debacle with Kitty, I had caught a glimpse of Beulah and Billy, standing in front of the machine shed with Slim Chance, right? Well, here's the part you might have missed…and, okay, maybe I missed it too because I had other things on my mind.

Let's reset the scene. Beulah was there. Billy was there. Who WASN'T there? Plato! Do you see the meaning of this? Wow, did I dare hope that she had finally come to her senses and ditched the King of Quail? Had she decided to take my advice?

I didn't dare hope, but I hoped anyway. But this time, I would try a different approach: slow, caring, tender, and sincere.

I hurried my pace and trotted up the hill. Tingles of excitement scampered down my backbone. I had a feeling that we were fixing to see the dawn in a new day in a new chapter in the book of my life in the Library of the Ages.

Yes siree, I had a feeling that good things were fixing to come my way.

Buttinski Butts In

I arrived in front of the machine shed and reconoodled the situation. Slim and Billy seemed to be involved in a serious conversation. I mean, they weren't laughing or goofing off, which went against their unusual pattern.

Beulah sat nearby and seemed...well, distant, distracted, but gorgeous. And I was pretty sure that she would be watching...well, ME.

I marched up to the men, pushed my way through and around their four legs, and took up a position between them. There, I announced my presence at the meeting. "Great news. I'm here! Sorry I'm late. Bring me up to speed. What's going on around here?"

I had expected...well, some kind of recognition,

if not an outpouring of joy then at least a "Hello, Hank" or "We had to start the meeting without you." I got nothing. They went right on talking.

That was okay, I'm not sensitive. A sensitive dog wouldn't last long on this outfit, but let's don't get started on that. I set my ears at Maximum Gathering Mode and listened. Soon, a pattern began to emerge.

1. Billy and Beulah had been driving across a pasture in a pickup.
2. Billy drove into hole, which high-centered the pickup.
3. The pickup was stuck in the pasture.
4. They had walked to our ranch to get help.

Oh, and one more thing. Billy said something else. He said, "I left my field jacket down by the creek with some dog food. Maybe he'll go to my scent." That made no scent to me, but that's what he said.

(A little more humor there. "Scent" instead of "sense." Ha ha. Not bad, huh?)

Okay, this brought me up to speed. I turned to Billy and delivered a bark. "You bet we can help, no problem. Let's get started. Can we pull it out with a four-wheel drive pickup, or do we need the tractor?"

Slim gave me a scowl. "Hank, hush." Gee,

what a grouch. Then he proceeded to repeat my exact words: "Can we pull it out with a four-wheel drive pickup, or do we need the tractor?"

What's the point in having a high-dollar cowdog on the place if they don't…oh well, at least he'd asked the right question.

Billy thought about it for a moment. "It's pretty well high-centered, but I think your pickup might do the job. We'll need a heavy chain or a nylon tow-rope."

Slim nodded. "We've got both." He started toward the machine shed and it wasn't my fault that he tripped over me. "Hank, for crying out loud!"

I turned an astonished glance at Billy. He chuckled. "He's kind of crabby in the fall, ain't he, pooch?"

Very crabby, and he didn't get much nicer in the spring either.

Slim fetched a nylon tow-rope and pitched it into the back of his pickup, then let down the tail-end gate. "Dogs in the back, load up!"

My heart thumped with joy. I would get to ride in the back of the pickup with the lovely Miss Beulah, just the two of us, all alone, on a drive through the countryside—without the annoying presence of her bird dog boyfriend, and without the almost-as-annoying presence of Drover.

Heh heh. My plan was proceeding like clockwurst.

Beulah came around to the rear of the pickup and our eyes met. "Hello, Hank."

Did you hear that? Holy smokes, for a moment, I couldn't draw a breath, and I stammered, "Heh-heh-hello, M-m-miss Buh-buh Bugle…Buford…Miss Beulah. Welcome to the ranch." Not a great start, all that stammering, but it got better. I swept a paw toward the pickup. "After you, ma'am."

She gave me a nod and a smile. I think she smiled. It was hard to tell. Maybe she didn't smile. As I said, she seemed distracted.

She hopped into the back of the pickup. I LEAPED into the back of the pickup, just the way a huge, graceful mule deer buck with a ten-point rack of antlers would leap over a five-strand barbed-wire fence.

We're talking about *very* athletic. A lot of mutts wouldn't have gone to the trouble of making a special presentation out of something as common as jumping into the back of a pickup. Me, I look at the Big Picture. Never pass up an opportunity to impress the ladies.

Did it work? Did she notice? Hard to say, but

I didn't let it get me down. We don't always catch a rabbit on the first run.

She settled herself against the cab at the front of the pickup bed. Her lovely dewberry eyes gazed off into the distance and the wind teased her flaxen hair. I was about to take my place beside her, when…

Huh? What was that? I heard a commotion behind me, as though something or someone were making a clumsy attempt to scramble into the back of the pickup—scratching and grunting.

I turned and was astonished to see…oh brother! It was Little Mister Buttinski, clawing his way into the middle of my private Valentine cruise with Miss Beulah. My vision went red, and it had nothing to do with the color of a box of Valentine candy. It had everything to do with being furious.

I whirled to the left and stomped toward the little wretch, just as he clawed his way into the bed of the pickup. I had every intention of pushing him out—out of the pickup and out of my life—but, well, I fell victim to a very unusual set of circumstances beyond my control.

See, just as I reached Buttinski and stood towering over him and was about to shove him out, Slim put the pickup in gear, goosed the accelerator, and popped the clutch. In other words, the pickup leaped forward. Drover was crawling on his cheating little belly, and guess who got tossed. Me.

Let me pause here to state something for the record. My getting tossed wasn't a random event. It wasn't just an unfortunate accident, one of those things that can happen on a working ranch. Don't forget who was driving: Slim Chance, a guy who never missed a chance to play childish pranks on his dogs.

We didn't have irreguffable proof in this case, but here's my suspicion. He was watching in the rearview mirror and saw that I was in a vulnerable position, so he seized the moment, goosed the pickup, and sent me flying.

That's exactly the kind of cheap trick he loves to pull on his dogs. When we're riding along in the cab and I'm sitting in the seat, minding my own business, he'll slam on the brakes and send me flying into the dashboard.

When I yawn—you might have trouble believing this, but it's true—when I yawn, he'll stick his finger into my mouth, ruining a good yawn and causing me to make urping sounds.

I'm not kidding. That's the kind of childish nonsense we dogs have to put up with around here, and rolling me out of the back of the pickup fit right into his pattern. I *know* he did it on purpose, and I'll bet he and Billy got a big laugh out of my misfortune.

I couldn't believe my lousy luck. I tumbled out of the back of the pickup and hit the ground like a load of hay. Oof! Did it hurt? You bet it hurt, knocked the wind right out of me. By the time I was able to regain my compottage, the pickup had traveled twenty yards down the road. Slim had shifted gears and was heading toward the mail box on the county road.

But here's the part that really hurt. The same little traitor who had snookered me into singing "Happy Birthday" to my worst enemy—that very same little twerp had cozied up beside Miss Beulah and was spouting poetry to her! I mean, he appeared to have lost his mind, what little he had left. How else can you explain his state of derangement—thinking that a sweet, dignified lady dog might have the slightest interest in hearing poetry from a shrimp like him?

Oh, cruel fate! Not only did I have to chase after the pickup that was carrying away the love of my life, but I had to listen to Drover's pathetic poetry at the same time! It was awful. It was embarrassing. It was so bad, I won't expose you to it. Don't even ask to hear his poem.

No.

Oh well, I guess it wouldn't hurt, but if you get sick or break out in a rash, don't blame me. I tried to warn you. Here's Exhibit A: Drover's silly poem:

Drover's Silly Poem

Oh gosh, holy cow, I can't believe my good luck,
To be riding alone in the back of a truck
With a beautiful lady,
Not Sally or Sadie,
But Beulah the Collie, by golly.

I wouldn't have dreamed this could happen to me,
It's twicer as nicer as scratching a flea.
And handier still,
Hank suffered a spill,
Leaving the two of us here, alone!

I hope you're enjoying my poem, Miss B.
I've been working on rhyming and verses,
you see.
And do I dare mention
My secret intention
Of starting a thousand-page novel next week?

Well, you heard it, what do you think? Actually, it was probably better than some of the drivel he'd composed in the past. At least this one had a few rhymes, but did you hear the part about him starting a "thousand-page novel next week?"

Ha. Drover couldn't even write his own name. He was doing well to make a paw print in the dust. It was such a huge whopper of a lie, it left me speechless, and even if I'd thought of some kind of response, I couldn't have said it, because, well, I was running to catch the pickup.

The question was...how would Miss Beulah respond? Would she rip into him for telling fibs in his poetry? Would she turn her back on him and refuse to speak to him for the rest of his life?

Or...this was almost unthinkable, but a guy has to face all possibilities...would she be swayed and swept off her feet by his goofball efforts as a troubadour?

Fellers, I had to catch the pickup and take care of business, before my love life went completely down the drain.

Plato, Lost Again!

I had been running pretty hard, but I had to run even faster. I rammed the throttle lever up to Turbo Six and went roaring down the road, with the scream of rocket engines filling my ears.

I closed the gap, and when Slim slowed down at the mailbox to make his turn onto the county road, I saw my opportunity. I flipped the switch to Raise Landing Gear and launched myself into the...

I never dreamed that Slim would be such a low-down skunk! See, he'd been watching me in the side mirror, and when he saw me Raise Gear and lift off the runway, he SLAMMED ON THE BRAKES! And you can imagine what that did.

The pickup stopped and I didn't.

Boy, you talk about a wreck. I crashed into the cab of the pickup so hard, it changed the shape of my nose. The good news was that I rolled Little Shakespeare and shut down his poetry. The bad news was that Miss Beulah took a tumble too, and when she picked herself up off the floor, she seemed, well, a little irritated.

"Oaf! What do you think you're doing? You knocked us down!"

"Beulah, I was trying to save you from a terrible fate."

"So...you crashed into us and knocked us down?"

"The driver slammed on the brakes, ma'am, and that wasn't my fault."

Her eyes were snapping-mad. "Well, are you sorry?"

"Absolutely. I'm very sorry that I knocked you down."

"And poor little Drover?"

"Poor little Drover should be prosecuted for inflicting his poetry on an innocent lady."

"I thought it was sweet. You, on the other hand, were rude, crude, and oafish."

"Very well, if you insist, I'll give him an apology." I shot a bullet-glare at the runt. He cringed and I whispered, "Go to your room.

WHAM!

Immediately!"

By that time, we were moving again, picking up speed. Drover gazed down at the road. "Well, if I jumped out now, it might break my neck."

"That will be fine, and the sooner the better." I turned back to Miss Beulah. "There. Drover and I have settled our differences."

She gave me a stony glare. "I didn't hear you say 'I'm sorry.'"

"Oh. Well, maybe the wind…"

"It wasn't the wind. You didn't say those two words—which seem very hard for you to say."

"Oh, all right." I turned back to The Poet. "Beulah insists that I give you a two-word message, so pay attention." I leaned toward his ear and whispered, "Happy birthday."

He grinned. "Gosh, thanks, but maybe you're thinking of Pete, 'cause you had to sing 'Happy Birthday' to him, remember?"

"Shhhhh!"

Too late. Beulah had heard and her stony glare had turned to ice. "Hank, say those two words, or I won't speak to you ever again."

Well, what's a dog to do when the love of his life threatens never to speak to him again? He does what is right and decent. I turned back to the little…to Drover, that is, to my Assistant

Head of Ranch Security. "All right, Drover, listen up. I've been ordered to say two words in your presence."

"Gosh, you brought me some birthday presents?"

"Will you please hush? This has nothing to do with birthdays. I said the wrong two words and I will now say the right two words, so pay attention."

"Boy, I get confused."

"Here are the right two words: Sorry I'm."

Drover gave me a blank stare. "I don't get it."

"That's fine, you don't have to get it." I whirled back to Miss Beulah. "There, I said the words and now..."

Oops. She was shaking her head. "You are SO stubborn, and this is SO silly! I have nothing more to add to this conversation." She turned her back to me and looked off into the distance.

"Beulah, be reasonable. I said the two words." Silence. "You didn't say they had to be in any particular order." Frigid silence. I gave Drover a scorching glare. "Now look what you've done!"

"Gosh, what did I do?"

"You...the list is so long, I can't even remember. Yes, I can. You've ruined my love life. She won't speak to me any more."

"Well, maybe I ought to do another poem. She

loved my first one."

"She hated your poem. It was so bad, it gave her a migraine headache and she needs some good verses to clean out her ears."

I pushed Drover aside and faced Miss Beulah. What I saw didn't look very promising. All the evidence suggested that...well, she was trying to ignore me. Could I deliver a poem that would thaw the glacier in her heart?

I had to try. I took a firm stance and cleared my throat.

My Wonderful Poem

Miss Beulah, beloved, behold a pure heart.
'Tis mine and not Drover's, and that's
where we start.
Okay, I'll be honest and admit a slight flaw.
See, saying 'I'm sorry' just sticks in my craw.

My strategy backfired, of that there's no
doubting.
You're mad as a hornet and seriously pouting.
But let me point out, before it gets worse,
My words were correct, only slightly reversed.

But that doesn't matter, for now you're
offended.
I offer this poem as a gift that will end it.

I'm sorry, I'm sorry, ten thousand times over,
The thousands for you and the ten are for
Drover.

So now that it's settled, let's go to Square One,
Let's bury the hatchets and have us some fun.
What matters the most is you didn't bring
Plato.
I'll miss him as much as...a rotten tomato!

Was that an awesome poem or what? You bet, totally awesome poem, and make no mistake, it came from the dregs of my heart. I waited to see if it would have the powerful effect I was hoping for.

I waited. For a long moment, she didn't move or make a sound, then her head shifted slightly and I saw her left eye peeking around at me. I heard her soft, honey-dripped voice. "You really do have a talent."

A blast of joy swept through my entire body. "Thank you, ma'am. As you know, I take pride in my verses. I'm not the kind of dog who," I shot a glance at Buttinski, "slops through a poem and says whatever rubbish comes to his mind."

Slowly, she turned to face me. She seemed to be wearing an odd smile. "I agree. Your rubbish is unique. It's so clever."

"Well, I'm honored and humbled and...wait. Did you say my 'rubbish'?" She nodded. "My 'rubbish' is clever? Is that what you said?" Her smile widened and she nodded again. "But surely there's been a mistake. See, 'rubbish' means..."

"Insincere? Glib? Superficial? Self-centered?"

"Yes ma'am, exactly, all of those things."

"Well, there you are. You have an amazing talent for balancing on the edge of sincerity and never putting in *even a toe*." She stepped forward and brought her long collie nose very close to mine. "Do you know why we got stuck in the pickup?"

"Uh...no. Billy drove into a hole?"

"We were out in the pasture, looking for Plato, and you had the nerve, the gall to call him a Rotten Tomato!" Tears flooded her eyes. "It's quail season and he's run off again! We've looked everywhere and can't find him. I'm so afraid..." She turned away and broke down crying.

I was shocked by this astounding twist in the story, and let's be honest. My first thought was to laugh out loud. I mean, how many times had we gone through this? It happened *every year* at quail season! The nincompoop took off looking for who-knows-what, got himself lost in the wilderness, and couldn't find his way back home.

And the girl of my dreams was bawling about it!

Well, my first thought might have been to laugh, but I slapped that idea right out of my mind. This was obviously the wrong time to laugh about Plato's Never-Ending Story. The rest of the world could laugh about it, but those of us in the pickup with Beulah had to bite our lips and put on a serious face.

I took a step toward her. "Beulah, don't cry. Surely he'll turn up."

She shook her head. "Always before, he's been lucky, but this time…sooner or later, the coyotes will find him." She gazed up at the sky. "I just don't understand why he does this!"

"Well, he's a bird dog."

"He's so sweet and kind, and most of the time, sensible."

"He's a bird dog. He has an incredible nose, hooked up to the brain of a…"

"Don't say it!" Her eyes flashed. "The poor thing takes spells. He's so…so gifted."

I clamped my jaws together. "Oh yes, gifted."

"And sometimes dogs with great talent seem… odd."

"Great word. I wouldn't have dared to speak it myself, but since you brought it up…yes, he's as odd as a square peg in a rubber duck."

"That doesn't make sense."

"That's my point. If he had any sense, he'd stop doing this stuff."

She narrowed her eyes. "Are you trying to make a joke out of this? Because if you are..."

"Beulah, all I'm saying is that...well, we should try to look at the brighter side."

She stared at me. "The brighter side!"

"Yes ma'am, absolutely. I mean, if he doesn't show up, we'll just have to trudge on without him." I gave her a wink. "And how'd you like to do a little trudging around with me, huh?"

Yipes. Maybe I should have waited to bring up The Brighter Side. I mean, there are times when a guy should shut his beak, right? This seemed to be one of those times. I knew it when her eyes flamed, her nostrils flared, and a torrent of air rushed into her lungs.

And in a tone of voice that would have taken the paint off the side of a barn, she screeched, "Heartless cad! If Plato doesn't come back, there will be no Brighter Side—ever! My last question to you is...*will you help us find him*?"

What! Me?

Hit By a Falling Asterisk

Well, Miss Beulah had pitched a tough question at me: Would I join the Search and Rescue mission to find her dingbat boyfriend?

"Of course I won't help you find him! If he happens to stumble back home, he'll be a wiser dog. If he doesn't, he'll get what he deserves."

"Heartless cad!" She whirled away and turned her back on me again.

Little Buttinski had been eavesdropping, so I turned to him. "She's being irrational."

"Yeah, but she nailed you on that one."

"What is that supposed to mean?"

"You're a heartless cad."

He whirled away and refused to speak to me. Oh brother. Well, it appeared that I had become an ugly toad, swimming around in the Punchbowl of Life, and had lost all my friends. But so what? When you're right, you don't need friends.

And besides, we had arrived at the spot in the pasture where Billy had gotten his pickup stuck, and it was time for me to go to work. At this point, the story shifts into a higher gear, so to speak, and gets pretty strange. See, nobody in our little group would have dreamed…well, you'll see.

Okay, let's set the scene. Whilst I was wasting my time in the back of the pickup, trying to give sensible advice to the collie dog who had once been the Lady of My Dreams, Slim had driven to the spot where Billy had…

Man alive, you talk about stuck! Billy had driven into a hole that was maybe two feet deep and had filled up level with tumbleweeds. Apparently he didn't see it until it was too late and the pickup had high-centered.

I hopped out of the back of the pickup and joined the men near the front of Billy's pickup. I didn't wish to seem pushy, but it was time for the Head of Ranch Security to step up and take charge.

I sized up the situation and began barking orders. "Slim, move your pickup around in front of Billy's."

"Hank, dry up."

"Let's connect the tow rope. Hook one end to the hitch ball on Slim's pickup and the other to the frame of..."

"Quit barking!"

Huh?

Slim towered over me and seemed, well, angry. Had he been yelling at ME? Hey, I was just trying to...

"If you want to bark, go down to the creek and bark at the frogs. Hush!"

Yes sir.

Frogs? Hmm, did he know that I had recently become an Ugly Toad in the Punch Bowl of Life? Was there a connection here? I mean, it seemed pretty interesting, frogs and toads coming up all of a sudden.

On the other hand, maybe it meant nothing. Skip it.

What a grouch. You know, it's very hard for us to help our people when they don't allow us to bark. What does that leave? Should we sing? Read them some poetry? Write them a letter on perfumed stationery? Sit there, wagging our tails?

This is the kind of thing a ranch dog has to

live with. Our people don't want to know what their dogs think. It's a crazy way to run a ranch, but there you are.

Even so, I'm proud to report that, after scolding me, Slim proceeded to put *my entire plan* into action, just as I had laid it out in my Barking Sequence. He connected the nylon tow rope to the hitch ball of his pickup and Billy tied the other end to the frame of his pickup.

Did I gloat or try to rub it in? No sir. I just sat there, trying to look humble. It seems to be very important for these guys to believe that they're running the show, and it's left to the dogs to show some maturity. I didn't utter a squeak, but you and I know the truth.

He used my plan.

When they'd gotten the pickups hooked together, Slim said, "I'll try to pull it easy. If that don't work, we'll go to Plan B, and you'd better hold on to your drawers, 'cause I'm going to back off and hit it hard."

Billy understood the plan. They went to their respective pickups and shifted both of them into four-wheel drive, low range. Slim's rig edged forward and took out the slack in the rope. He let out on the clutch and leaned into the effort. Both pickup motors roared, and on both vehicles, the front and back tires threw up dirt and grass. Plan A had flopped.

I rushed over to the front of Billy's pickup and began barking. "This isn't working. Go to Plan B. Repeat, Plan B. Slim, you're going to have to back off and give it a jerk. Let's go, we're burning daylight."

Slim was watching me in his side mirror. He grinned and shook his head. Fine, he could grin all he wanted, and I gave him another bark. "Stop messing around and let's get this done!"

Slim backed up a few feet and shifted into first gear. He stuck his arm out the window and moved his hand in a circle. I guess that meant, "Hold on to your drawers." He gunned the motor, popped the clutch, and the pickup leaped forward.

Under pressure, a nylon rope will stretch like a rubber band, which is just what we wanted. A stretched rope will add to the pull-power of the so-forth. What you never expect in these situations is that, under heavy tension, the loop might slip off the hitch ball . When that happens, it's Katie, Bar the Door.

I don't want to scare anyone, but...well, it happened. Slim's pickup lunged forward. The nylon tow rope stretched and stretched...and came back like a rubber band. The rope went flying toward the front of Billy's pickup, as though it had been fired from a giant sling-shot. Bammo!

Guess who was standing near the front of Billy's pickup. Me. I'd been supervising, remember? And guess who got creamed—and we're talking about wiped out—by the tow rope. Me. I never saw it coming and, fellers, it knocked me for a loop. I thought I'd been hit by a truck or a falling asterisk. Askeroid. Asteroid, there we go.

Actually, it happened so fast, I didn't *think* anything. It must have knocked me out, because... you know what? At this point in the story, I must let you in on a piece of crucial information. Without it, you won't be able to make much sense out of what comes next.

Here's the deal. That rope whacked me so hard, it knocked me out, cold, and made me... well, a little goofy, might as well go straight to the point. The next thing I knew, I was lying in the grass and looking up at a circle of worried faces: two men dressed in cowboy clothes and two dogs. I didn't recognize any of them.

The first cowboy said, "Well, he's breathing. Man alive, that thing hit him like a cannonball. I thought we'd lost him."

The second cowboy nodded. "Yeah, it would

have killed a good dog. Hank, can you stand up? Come on, pooch, test out your legs."

He had called me "Hank." I wasn't "Hank" and didn't know anyone named "Hank," but he wanted me to stand up and test my legs, so I struggled to my feet and tested my legs.

They didn't work too well. I stood up, wobbled, staggered a few steps, and fell into the lap of one of the dogs—a lady dog, it appeared, with a long, handsome nose, amazing ears, and a pair of brown eyes that seemed a bit sad.

She was a collie and…my goodness, gorgeous!

"Pardon me, m'lady, I'm having a little trouble with my balance."

"I'm not surprised. You're just lucky to be alive."

My eyes feasted on her beauty. "Indeed, and here I am, not merely alive, but sitting in thy lap. 'Tis more than I could have wished for which to have wished. May I inquire about thy name?"

She gave me a puzzled look. "My name, as you very well know, is Beulah."

"Ah! Lady Beulah, how sweet it is to meet thee, and to have tumbled into thy lap! Methinks I shant wish to leave this pleasant spot."

"Hank? Are you all right?"

"More than all right, and allow me to introduce

myself." I struggled to my feet and dipped my head. "I know not this 'Hank' of whom thou speakest. I am Sir Barksalot, Knight of the Kitchen Table. I place myself at thy service."

There was a long moment of silence, then she said, "I'm not sure I understand. Does it mean you've changed your attitude? You'll help us find poor Plato?"

"If finding Purpluto would please thee, then it shall be done. Thy wish is my command and guiding star."

"Are you making fun?"

"Not yet, m'lady. All things in their time." I dared to give her a wolfish smile. "First we serve the lady's wish, then we see to the fun. Now, if thou wouldst excuse me, I shall depart on my mission."

She turned to the other dog. "Drover, he doesn't seem normal."

Rover shrugged. "Yeah, maybe getting socked by the rope made him a little..." He rolled his eyes around.

She nodded. "I agree, but if he can help us find poor Plato...maybe you should go with him. He might need some help."

"Me? Well, I'd love to, Miss Beulah, but you know, this old leg has really been giving me fits."

He limped in a circle. “See? Terrible pain. It hit me in the night. Oh, my leg!”

She beamed him a glare. “Drover, stop it! Try to be helpful.”

“Oh drat. Yes ma’am, I’ll do what I can.”

Lady Beulah turned her pleading gaze on me. Even with the sadness in her eyes, her beauty overwhelmed me with overwhelmness. She said, “You seem a little rattled.”

“Thank you, m’lady. Tis an honor to be rattled in thy service.”

“Drover will go with you. Help us find poor Plato, please!”

“Lady Beulah, if Purpluto can be found, find him I shall. Until we meet again…” I gave her a bow and shot a stern glare at her muttish little friend. “You. Page. Come along.”

This is pretty strange, isn’t it? But strange things can happen when a guy gets knocked in the head. I guess you’d better keep reading.

Another Kitty Conspiracy

And so it was that I left Lady Beulah and began my long journey into the…you know, I was fuzzy in the head and my legs were still a little soggy. In other words, I had a trouble walking in a straight line and, well, had no idea where we were going on this crusade.

The little pooch, Rover, was tagging along behind me, so I waited for him to catch up. He gave me a peculiar look. "Hank, you're acting kind of weird."

"I feeleth somewhat weird, but why doest thou continue calling me 'Hank'?"

"'Cause that's who you are, and it's really weird that you've forgotten everything. Remember the gas tanks?"

"Nay."

"Emerald Pond?"

"Nay."

"Pete?"

A faint memory stirred in my mind. "A disease?"

"Oh boy, this is really bad. Maybe we'd better go home and let you rest a while. I think that rope messed you up."

"Home? Rest? Tis not possible, for I hath promised my service to Lady Beulah. Rover, thou hast become my page, it seemeth, although thy shriveled body dost not inspire great confidence."

"Thanks, but my name's Drover, Drover with a D."

"Thy name, O Worm, shall be whatever I chooseth to call thee, and henceforth thy name shall be Rover Without a D."

"Oh well, it's only one letter, and what's one letter on a page?" He snickered.

Silence engulfed us. "Why snickerest thou?"

"Well, it was kind of a joke. See, you called me your page, and what's one letter on a page? Hee hee. Get it?"

I looked off into the distance and gave my head a shake. The fogginess was still bothering me, and so was this little mutt. "Henceforth, refrain from levity."

"Yeah, it really pulls me down."

"Pardon?"

"Gravity. It pulls me down."

"Indeed." I turned my gaze to the country ahead of us, rolling prairie intersected by a tree-lined creek. "Page, bring my horse and sword, and sound the trumpets. Alert the men that our solemn mission for Lady Beulah hath begun to begin."

A column of knights assembled. Trumpets blared and banners unfurled, and we set out on our mission to find...whoever he was, some guy with an odd name. Purpluto.

It was quite a scene—bright-colored banners flapping in the breeze, hundreds of gallant knights dressed in shining armor, armed with swords and lances, and mounted on prancing horses.

I took my place at the front of the column, of course, accompanied by my page who was riding upon a donkey. His name was Rover Without a D—my page, that is, not the donkey.

We had ridden several miles in splendor when, once again, I noticed the foggy feeling in my head...and suddenly realized that I had no idea what we were doing.

I halted the column. "Page, art thou aware of where we goeth on our crusade?"

"Well, sort of. We're looking for a bird dog."

"A bird or a dog?"

"Well, he's a dog that points birds."

"That seemeth pointless."

"Well, that's what he does. Oh, and every year during bird season, he runs off and gets lost. I guess we're supposed to find him."

"Ah yes, and this would be Purpluto?"

"No, his name's Plato, but Beulah always calls him poor Plato."

"Perplexing." I took a closer look at my page and noticed an important detail. "What happened to your donkey?"

"What donkey?"

"You were riding on a donkey. You stuck a feather in his cap and called him Macaroni, but he's gone, vanished." The fog in my head seemed to be lifting. "Good grief, someone around here is stealing donkeys! Bark the alarm!" I delivered several loud, stern barks, then noticed another astonishing detail. The column of knights had also vanished. "Drover, what's going on around here?"

"Hey, you called me Drover."

"Of course I called you Drover. That's your name. The donkey was Macaroni and..." I blinked my eyes and gave my head a shake. "Where are we and what are we doing? Facts, Drover, I need facts."

Drover rolled his eyes around and plunked his little bohunkus on the ground. "Well, this is going to take some time. Slim was pulling Billy's pickup out of a hole..."

"Wait, who's Slim? Do I know him?"

"Yeah, he's the guy who makes boiled turkey necks."

"Boiled turkey necks? That's ridiculous...no, wait, it's coming back to me. He eats them, right? Okay, he was pulling a turkey neck out of a hole?"

"No, he was pulling a pickup out of a hole and the rope stretched like a rubber band. It came loose and whacked you in the head. It knocked you silly, and when you woke up, you said you were Sir Barksalot, Knight of the Kitchen Table."

"I said that? Sir Barksalot?" I paced a few steps away and tried to sweep the scattered crumbs of thought into a neat little pile. "Okay, I'm starting to see a pattern here. I received a blow to the head and suffered a spell of tunisia."

"I knew something was fishy."

"Apparently I lost my memory. How long have I been in this state?"

"You've been in Texas all your life."

"When did I get the blow on my head?"

"Oh, about an hour ago."

"And I promised Beulah that I would find

Plato?"

"Yep, you sure did."

"I can't believe this." I paced back over to him. "I won't do it. Why should I? The dog's an imbecile."

"Yeah, but you promised you would, and it wasn't just a little bitty promise."

"How big was it?"

"Oh, four feet long and three feet wide."

"That's a big promise. If I welched on it, she'd probably never speak to me again."

"I bet you're right."

I cut my eyes from side to side. "Wait a second. That word just released a covey of memories in my head. 'Bet.' Have we done any betting lately?"

His gaze drifted away. "Oops."

I began pacing a circle around him, as I often do when I'm pursuing the fireflies of truth. "Yes, yes. A picture is forming. I see two dogs and a cat. You were there. It was somebody's birthday, right?" He nodded. "And the cat was Pete, right?" He nodded. "And we were making some kind of wager?"

"I need to go home." He got up to leave.

"Sit down, son, it's all coming back to me. Two dogs and a cat. I can almost hear their voices. They're saying…" I whirled around to face him.

"Yes, of course! Don't you get it? The cat was betting that I would break my promise to Miss Beulah, that I wouldn't help her find Plato. He was betting against me!"

Drover stared at me. "I'll be derned."

"Ha ha! Oh, this is delicious. You see, Drover, I'll do anything to wreck the cat, even if it means helping Plato. Why are you crossing your eyes again?"

"I'm confused."

"Well, snap out of it. We're fixing to go find a bird dog."

"I need to visit the weeds."

"Make it snappy."

Drover scampered off into a wild plum thicket nearby. He's so predictable. Any time we have a deadline to make, any time we're about to embark upon a new adventure, he has to "go visit the weeds." Oh well, if he didn't visit the weeds, he might do something worse.

I paced and waited. Precious time was slipping away, and I could almost hear the tock clocking. "Hurry up." No response. "Drover, we need to launch the mission. Drover?" Silence. "Drover, if you don't come out immediately, I will come get you."

He didn't appear, so I plunged into the thicket and…ouch, got scratched by several thorns. They have thorns, you know, those wild plum bushes. They're not as bad as mesquite thorns, but they will get your attention.

But the important detail here is that I found no sign of Drover, not even a wet spot in the sand. In other words, the little slacker had… oh brother!

I Find Him

Didn't I say that Drover is predictable? He is SO predictable. Give him a job that involves even the slightest mention of danger or work, and he will head to the barn like a spoiled horse, like a homing pigeon, like an…I don't know what.

I would like to report that I didn't care, but maybe I did. Of course I did! Hey, I was still recovering from a head injury that had left me a little daffy. Remember all that stuff about Sir Barksalot, Knight of the Kitchen Table? That was Weird with a Capital B. Dogs who make up stuff like that have no business going out alone on a dangerous mission.

And speaking of that mission…in a moment of weakness, I had promised to find my second-worst enemy in the world, the same bird merchant who had stolen away my collie girlfriend.

Did I want to find him? NO. Did I want to save his bacon again? NO. But was I honor-bound to go looking for him? It had to be done.

It *would* be done, but not with a cheerful heart. Just because you honor a promise doesn't mean you have to be nice about it. I had every intention of NOT being nice about it.

I ran my gaze around in a circle and realized… gulp…I was all alone in the Wild West, in a trackless wilderness, miles away from the nearest outpost of civilization. I had only a vague sense of my present location (somewhere east of our ranch headquarters and somewhere west of Billy's ranch), and I was supposed to be looking for a lost dog, whose location was even more of a mystery than my own.

Wait! Back at the machine shed, Billy had said something that didn't make sense at the time, but now…

Do you remember this? Okay, pay attention. Billy said that he'd left his field jacket down near the creek, right? With some dog food, and then he said, "Maybe he'll come to my scent."

Boy, it's amazing what a dog can do when he's playing with a full deck. Of course! Billy had used an old quail hunter's trick. Don't you get it? When an idiot bird dog runs off and gets lost (it happens all the time), the hunter leaves an article of clothing that holds the familiar scent of the man—a field jacket. Of course!

See, a bird dog doesn't have a normal brain, but he's got an incredible nose, and we're talking about a piece of equipment that can locate a flea in a thousand-acre pasture. He might sniff around for half a day, lost in his own little bird-world, but eventually, he'll pick up the familiar scent of his master. He'll go to the jacket and wait for someone to find him, and while he's there, he'll have groceries, so he won't starve.

Well, this important clue promised to send the case plunging in an entirely new direction. If I could locate Billy's jacket, I might find the dog. And if I found the nitwit, I just might score some big points with the Lady of My Dreams.

It was worth a try, because...well, all my other efforts to win her heart had ended up like bugs splattered on the Windshield of Life. I don't mean to whine about this, but I can tell you that it had been very discouraging.

So, with a plan firmly in mind, I headed south in a long trot. Why south? Because I was north of the creek, which means that the creek lay to the south. I could see the tree-lined profile of the creek about half a mile in front of me.

By the way, "front" always means south unless you're heading north, in which case you have to recobbulate your instruments to show that "front" means north.

Navigation out in the wilderness is pretty tricky and you really have to pay attention to those instruments.

Anyway, I headed south, toward the line of cottonwood trees and native elms that wound like a big snake through the prairie country. When I reached the north bank, I did a thorough scan of the area and found...well, trees on both sides of the creek, pretty muchly what you'd expect. But no sign of Billy's field jacket or the Birdly Wonder.

Here, I faced a decision. Would I pursue my search to the left or to the right? It was a tough decision and also pretty crucial, because if I went left and that was right, I would find him, whereas if I went right and that was wrong, I wouldn't.

After doing a few calculations in my head (which had a painful knot on the top, by the way), after doing the so-forth, I came up with an answer. It would be lefter to go left but righter to go right, and we should always try to do the right thing, so by George, there was nothing left to do but to go right.

It's pretty amazing what I was able to do with higher mathematics, isn't it? You bet. Ordinary mutts don't even attempt it, but when you're Head of Ranch Security, you have to crack the whip on those numbers and make 'em pull the pudding.

I punched the numbers into the Guidance System, executed a sharp turn to the left, and made my way down the creek. As I walked, I swept the country in front of me with VizRad (visual radar) and pulled in a steady stream of information.

Here's one item of information that turned up pretty quickly: no frogs. This was a matter of special interest because, if you recall, that very afternoon, Slim had delivered a rude, smart-mouth remark to me: "If you want to bark at something, go down to the creek and bark at the frogs."

Well, the data we were collecting along the creek completely destroyed his Theory of Frogs. *There weren't any frogs along the creek in November*, and do you know why? Because when it gets cold, they dig into the mud and sleep all winter. It's a process called…

I don't remember what it's called, but *frogs know* and that's all that matters. If you want to know about frogs, don't ask Slim. Ask a frog, because nobody knows more about being a frog than a frog.

Sorry, I didn't mean to get so emotional.

Where were we? Oh yes, looking for the Birdly Wonder. In that department, I wasn't doing so well—no sign, no tracks, no nothing. But then...I came to a sudden stop and zoomed in on some kind of object that didn't match the colors of the surrounding country. The coordinates flashed across the screen of my mind.

Distance: fifty yards.

Bearing: zero-five-chubby-checker.

Description: indistinct white something with dark spots.

Affiliation: probably friendly, but who knows?

Plan: approach with caution.

I moved to the left, away from the creek bank, and began creeping through the cover of some willows and tall weeds. In Stealthy Crouch Mode, I crept forward another twenty-five yards, and there I began picking up sounds—growling sounds. I halted the column and scoped it out.

Okay, good news. The object we were picking up on VizRad turned out to be Plato. Apparently he had caught the scent of his master's field jacket and had stayed with the jacket, just as Billy had hoped. But here was the puzzle: what was all the growling about, and what was he doing?

I scoped the entire area once again, just to be sure this wasn't a trap that had been set by the cannibals. Those guys are dumber than dirt, but it doesn't pay to get careless. The area appeared to be secure, so I crept forward. The growling sounds grew louder. What on earth was he doing?

Ten yards from the subject, I halted and announced myself. "Security Division, Special Crimes Unit! What's going on here?"

You know, I really enjoy doing this, especially when the subject thinks he's all alone in the world and is doing something ridiculous. It always wakes 'em up.

You'd have thought that he'd stuck his nose into an electrical socket. He jumped three feet into the air and appeared to be trying to swim or fly, but he returned to the earth with a crash and stared at me with eyes that resembled paper plates—white circles with a tiny dots in the center.

"What…who…Hank, is that you? By golly, I had no idea, I mean, you just came out of nowhere!"

"Ten-four on that." I walked over to the jacket

and studied the evidence. The jacket had been torn to shreds. "What's going on here?"

"Well, Hank, by golly, it's kind of a long story."

"Talk."

He scowled and tightened his mouth. "We were hunting birds, Hank, great day, coveys everywhere, some bobwhites but mostly blue quail. And you know how they are."

"Who?"

"The blue quail. They won't give you a decent covey-rise. It's so frustrating! They run."

"So you took off after a bunch of blue quail... and got lost?"

He squinted his eyes and twisted his mouth. "I believe that might be...yes. And Hank, let me be frank. It's so embarrassing when this happens. I mean, I was on them, but those blues kept running and, well, they just disappeared. The darned things can do that, just vanish. And Hank, I looked around..."

"And you had no idea where you were."

"Right, exactly. And Hank, I must confide in you." His head sank. "This has happened before."

"No kidding? This has happened before?" I stormed over to him and glared into the vacuum of his eyes. "Why am I not surprised? Listen, Bird Brain, we go through this every year, and

I'm always the one who has to find you."

"I'm so ashamed."

"Then why do you keep doing it?"

"Honestly, Hank, I don't know. It seems irrational, doesn't it?"

"No, it's worse than that, but never mind. Go on with your story. You managed to find your master's field jacket."

"I did, yes, you're exactly right, Hank, and that seems to be the only smart thing I did all day. The scent brought back comfortable memories and, you know, reminded me of…home."

"The same home you keep running away from?"

"Yes, right, the very same one."

"Okay, here's the big question. If the scent reminded you of home…why were you tearing the jacket to shreds when I walked up?"

He stared at me with his mouth hanging open. You won't believe what he said. I guarantee you won't believe it.

The Secret Pledge Is Revealed

Okay, I had just dropped the Big Question on Plato: why was he ripping his master's field jacket to shreds when I walked up and caught him in the act?

A puzzled look drifted over his face. "Well, Hank, isn't it obvious?"

"No, it's not obvious at all. I can't imagine. Tell me."

"Well, I was…I was hungry, starving, in fact, famished. Listen, Hank, I'd been running quail for hours. Have you ever calculated how many calories we use in the field?"

"No."

"Well, I can tell you, it's an enormous number, and I was starving."

"Starving. So let me get this right. You were so hungry, you tried to eat a field jacket?"

"Well, I…it sounds ridiculous when you put it that way."

"Then what were you doing?"

His eyes drifted to the horizon. "I wasn't exactly trying to eat it, Hank. It's more complicated than that. May I go straight to the point?"

"Yes, let's try that."

"I know this must be frustrating to you, Hank."

"Will you hurry up?"

His gaze drifted up to the clouds. "Right. You see, there seems to be some mechanism that's activated when I'm very hungry."

"Keep going."

"Hank, when I get extremely hungry, I seem prone to…oh me…to odd behavior, you might say. Am I making myself clear?"

I stuck my nose in his face. "Did it ever enter your flea's brain that THERE WAS A BOWL OF DOG FOOD SITTING ON TOP OF THE COAT?"

His eyes went blank. "You're joking."

"I'm not joking."

"A bowl of dog food?"

"Yes, sitting in plain sight on top of the coat." I pointed to a metal bowl near the coat. "That's the bowl." I pointed to a scatter of dog food kernels on the ground. "That's the dog food."

He went to the scatter of kernels and sniffed it. "You're right, Hank, that's dog food."

"Your master left it here so you wouldn't starve to death while you were running away from your happy home and feeling lonesome about it. And what did you do? You tried to eat the coat!"

He seemed on the virgil of tears. "I'm so ashamed, Hank, so ashamed!"

"Good. Now help me out, pal. You've got the best bird-dog nose in Texas, but you couldn't smell a bowl of dog food right in front of your face? How can that happen?"

He shook his head. "I…I…I can't explain it, Hank, but it does solve one part of the mystery."

"What mystery?"

"Why the skunk was here."

There was a long moment of silence as I tried to absorb this. "You saw a skunk?"

"Right, yes. When I arrived at the jacket… and Hank, let me repeat that I was exhausted, dehydrated, and weak from hunger. When I arrived, I found a skunk…eating something."

"The dog food."

"Right, exactly, but I never thought about… anyway, I shooed him away and started chewing the…well, the jacket."

"Oh brother."

He paced a few steps away. "Of course! It was a circuitry issue. The odor of a skunk overwhelmed all the wiring patterns." He took a deep breath and blinked his eyes. "Hank, I'm feeling better about this. It's comforting to know that there's an answer."

Who can stay mad at a dog like this? I found myself smiling. "Plato, you're one of a kind. What I don't understand is...why is Beulah so fond of you? I don't want to sound harsh, but you're such a dingbat!"

He was quiet for a moment. "I hear what you're saying, Hank, I really do, but...there are secrets."

"Secrets?"

"Yes. You see," a distant look came into his eyes, "I was orphaned as a pup. I ran wild, lived from day to day on what I could beg and steal. But then an elderly lady-dog found me in the gutter and took me home. Hank, she found something in me to love and tried to protect me from this...this crazy bird-dog side of my nature. Because of her, I'm alive today."

"I didn't know."

"There's more. On her deathbed, she made her niece promise to look after me and carry on

the tradition." He looked into my eyes. "Hank, the dear woman who cared for me was...*Beulah's Aunt Gertie*!"

"And she made Beulah promise..."

"Yes. For years she's been my protector, and words can't express my gratitude. But it's not right, Hank. I must release her from the pledge." He hung his head. "She likes you, Hank, I know she does. You're brave and resourceful. You have all the great qualities I lack."

"Don't be too hard on yourself."

"No, I'm being honest. You've been right about me all along. I'm just a skinny, stick-tailed bird dog buffoon who points tennis shoes, chases birds, and gets lost. She deserves better."

I paced away from him and tried to make sense of all this. "Plato, I never thought I'd hear such a sensible remark come out of your mouth. You're right."

"I hope we can still be friends."

I marched over to him and laid a paw across his shoulder. "Friends forever, pal, friends to the bone."

"You won't tell her about the…you know, me eating the jacket, will you?"

I laughed. "No, that'll be our secret."

"Thanks, Hank. It's so ridiculous, I wouldn't want anyone to know." He glanced around and blinked his eyes. "Well, maybe we should get me back home. They'll be worried. But I'll be honest, Hank, I have no idea where we are."

"Leave it to me, pal. Just sit back and enjoy the scenery."

"Great." He started walking off in the wrong direction. "You know, Hank, I feel as though…"

"Hey! Stop! Turn around! Follow me."

"Oh, sorry."

"Stay behind me and don't wander off."

"Right. I'll stay directly behind you, Hank, and this time, I'm going to pay attention."

We set out on our journey, heading east down the creek. By then, I had figured out that Billy's place was on this same creek and all we had to do was follow it for a mile or so downstream. I took the lead and Plato tagged along behind, gazing at the scenery and babbling.

"As I was saying, Hank, I feel as though a heavy burden has been lifted from my shoulders—all those years, living with guilt and feeling like an imposter. Now it's flown away like…Hank, do you smell something?"

"Yes, Plato, I smell fallen leaves, creek water, and dirt."

"No, I mean something different, unusual."

"Turn off your nose, stay in line, follow me, and don't get lost."

"Right. I agree, Hank. You're always so sensible."

Whew! Saving that guy from himself was an ordeal, but we didn't have much farther to go. If I could just get him back home…mercy, I could almost see the sparkle in her eyes when she got the news that *she was free from her pledge*!

But just then, something dreadful happened.

I ran into someone into whom I shouldn't have run into whom. You'll never guess, but I'll give you a hint.

He was bad news.

A Mixed Ending

Holy smokes, Plato had decided to release Beulah from her pledge, which pretty muchly cleared the way for my schemes and ambitions. I didn't wish him any bad luck, but don't forget what he'd said: *She deserved better.*

That had come from his own mouth and it was true. She deserved...well, ME.

As you can imagine, my spirits were soaring, and my mind was filled with the most pleasant...

Remember that skunk Plato had mentioned? I hadn't given it much thought, but I should have, because I walked right into him. I was shocked and so was he. He stared at me with those dark, beady little skunk-eyes, and...well, what do you suppose a normal, healthy American dog does when he comes face-to-face with a skunk with beady eyes?

He barks, of course. Without a thought, I gave him my best Train Horns Bark. BWONK! Bad call. Never do Train Horns when your nose is three inches from a skunk.

What came next was a blur of rapid motion and bad memories. The skunk whipped around and blasted me with yucky yellow poison, and we're talking about toxic material that would gag a buzzard.

I gasped for air and staggered in circles. I was blinded by the stuff and could hardly breathe. Behind me, I heard a voice. "By golly, Hank, was

that a skunk? You know, I thought I smelled something back there. Boy, that was bad luck, wasn't it?"

I gagged and gasped and did Dives in the Grass to rid myself to the awful stuff. At last, I was able to open my eyes, and what do you suppose I saw? The face of a bird dog.

"If you smelled something, why didn't you tell me?"

"Well, Hank, I wasn't a hundred percent positive and, you know, I was enjoying the fall foliage. The elms are really amazing. I don't notice them when I'm on a hunt." He approached me with slow steps, sniffing. He stopped. "Oh Hank, this is pretty bad. No, it's *real* bad. You took a direct hit."

"No kidding? I hardly noticed."

"I guess you're joking, Hank, and I must tell you, that's one of the things I've always admired..."

"Never mind. Let's get out of here."

"Hank, I feel personally responsible for this. I should have..."

"Will you please dry up?"

Maybe I shouldn't have snarled at him. He wasn't a bad guy, but a big mouth will overwhelm a good heart every time. The guy talked too much.

So off we went on the last leg of our journey. Plato continued to babble about the fall foliage and, for a while, I was almost paralyzed by the stench. I mean, that hateful little squirt-bomb had really messed me up.

But you know, time hath its own cure for skunk musk. At first, it's awful, but after a while, the old nose gets over-loaded and quits working. By the time we reached Beulah's place, everything seemed pretty muchly back to normal.

When we entered the headquarters compound of Billy's ranch, I halted the column. Up ahead, I saw a modest ranch house, a barn, corrals, a saddle shed, a tractor, all the stuff you'd expect to see on a Texas ranch.

I looked closer and…there she was, sitting beneath a large cottonwood tree whose yellow leaves were sparkling in the sun. She seemed anxious, glancing around and waiting for our return. Then…she saw us.

I took command. "Plato, you go first and explain the situation. I'll wait here."

"Right, good plan, Hank. Beulah and I will need a little time to ourselves, and I must tell you, Hank, this isn't going to be…"

I stuck my nose in his face. "Go. Take care of business. Quit yapping."

"Right, I totally agree." He made a sour face and fanned the air. "Oooo!"

He headed toward Beulah in an awkward gait, I mean, the guy couldn't even run straight. He was all legs and tail, with tongue and ears flapping in the breeze. He called out, "Honey Bunch!" And she answered with, "Plato, you're back!" She ran toward him and they met. They spoke in whispers, laughed, and...I didn't like this part...they nuzzled.

Oh well, that was about to change.

They spoke in low voices and seemed to be arguing. Then Plato's voice rang out. "No, Sugar Cakes, it's final. I insist."

Heh heh. That sounded better.

She started toward me, and, fellers, my old heart went to work like a whole drum section. Closer and closer she came. Her gaze lifted and came to me, and I could see the flickering flames of Love dancing in her eyes. And did I mention the music? Yes, I began hearing a beautiful, tender song—Our Song.

My breaths were coming hard and fast now, and with only ten feet of space between us, she stopped and gave me a smile that lit up the whole world.

"Hello, Hank."

"Hello, Beulah. You look stunning."

"Thank you, and you look…rather handsome."

"Beulah, I've never felt handsomer in my whole life."

"I guess Plato told you about our secret."

"Yes ma'am, and it explains a lot. You know, Beulah, I could never understand…"

"Shh! I won't have you saying unkind things about him."

"Sorry. He's weird but never mind. The important thing is the pledge."

She nodded. "Yes. He released me from the pledge I made to my…" Her voice quivered. "…to my poor Aunt Gertie in her last hour. She was so fond of him!"

"Right, but the bottom line is that we're moving on to better things."

"Maybe. Yes."

"And, well, I've brought him home again, and I know how grateful you must be."

"I'm very grateful. Thank you."

"And while you're in such a grateful mood, maybe we should talk about…well, US." I wiggled my left eyebrow. "This could be a new beginning, right?"

"It could be, Hank. I…I just don't know. This is all new and strange."

"Well, hey, here's some great news. I'm neither one—new or strange. And here's an idea. How's about me and you...well, getting reacquainted, shall we say?"

The silence between us throbbed. Then...she smiled and whispered, "I suppose we could try."

Holy smokes! Have you ever seen a herd of cattle stampeding through an open gate? That was me, fellers. I became a whole stampede, all by myself, and we're talking about thundering hooves and gate posts snapping off at the roots.

I dashed into her awaiting arms and...huh?

She screamed. And I mean SCREAMED and gave me a shove and backed away with...wow... with a really crazy look in her eyes. And she said, "What have you done!"

I was speechless for a moment. "What have I done? I just brought your nitwit boyfriend back home, rescued you from a ridiculous pledge, and I'm here to collect my reward."

"Well, mister, you won't collect any rewards when you show up smelling like...like a GARBAGE DUMP!"

"A garbage...oh, wait, it was only a skunk."

Her eyes flamed. "Only a skunk! You smell horrible! You stink! How could you...ohhhh!" She stamped her foot.

"Beulah, try to be reasonable. Hey, how about another poem?"

"HOW ABOUT A BATH!"

"A bath? I'm kind of busy right now."

She shook her head. "I can't believe this. I can NOT...Well! Thank you for all your help and maybe you can come back another time."

"What? You mean..."

"When you haven't been playing with skunks!"

Her collie nose went straight up in the air, she whirled around, and marched right back to...oh brother! She went back to the Birdly Wonder!

And what did he do? He shrugged his shoulders and gave me a big sloppy grin and yelled, "By golly, Hank, what can I say? Bad luck, but thanks for everything and have a great day!"

I did an about-face and marched away from this...this mutter-mumble fulmination of foddling fiddle sticks boiling in the ominous phooey. I was so mad, I hardly noticed the hundred pieces of my shattered heart that lay like broken glass in the bottom of my phooey.

Oh well, I didn't care. Let her have the moron, and speaking of morons, if he was such a moron, how come I had walked into the skunk and he hadn't? And how come I was going home ALONE and he was...never mind.

The point is that I had suffered a minor setback in my quest for Beulah's undying love, but after a few days' rest and a bath or two, I would return to the fight—an older dog, a wiser dog, a dog who had been tempered by fire and hardship.

That three-mile trudge back to ranch headquarters wasn't fun, but I got it done, and things improved when I arrived. Right away, I located the cat and ran him up a tree, then went looking for little Buttinski. I found him hiding in the machine shed, gave him a quick court-martial, and put his nose in the corner for a whole hour, exactly where it belonged.

I sat beside his prison cell and listened to him complain about the skunk smell, and as icing on the punch, I made him sing "Happy Birthday" to ME. It wasn't my birthday, but I didn't care.

Happy birthday, happy ending. This case is closed, but by George, I SHALL RETURN!

Have you read all of Hank's adventures?

1 *The Original Adventures of Hank the Cowdog*
2 *The Further Adventures of Hank the Cowdog*
3 *It's a Dog's Life*
4 *Murder in the Middle Pasture*
5 *Faded Love*
6 *Let Sleeping Dogs Lie*
7 *The Curse of the Incredible Priceless Corncob*
8 *The Case of the One-Eyed Killer Stud Horse*
9 *The Case of the Halloween Ghost*
10 *Every Dog Has His Day*
11 *Lost in the Dark Unchanted Forest*
12 *The Case of the Fiddle-Playing Fox*
13 *The Wounded Buzzard on Christmas Eve*
14 *Hank the Cowdog and Monkey Business*
15 *The Case of the Missing Cat*
16 *Lost in the Blinded Blizzard*
17 *The Case of the Car-Barkaholic Dog*

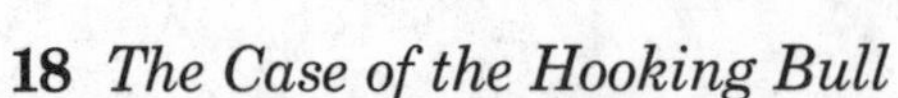

18 *The Case of the Hooking Bull*
19 *The Case of the Midnight Rustler*
20 *The Phantom in the Mirror*
21 *The Case of the Vampire Cat*
22 *The Case of the Double Bumblebee Sting*
23 *Moonlight Madness*
24 *The Case of the Black-Hooded Hangmans*
25 *The Case of the Swirling Killer Tornado*
26 *The Case of the Kidnapped Collie*
27 *The Case of the Night-Stalking Bone Monster*
28 *The Mopwater Files*
29 *The Case of the Vampire Vacuum Sweeper*
30 *The Case of the Haystack Kitties*
31 *The Case of the Vanishing Fishhook*
32 *The Garbage Monster from Outer Space*
33 *The Case of the Measled Cowboy*
34 *Slim's Good-bye*
35 *The Case of the Saddle House Robbery*
36 *The Case of the Raging Rottweiler*
37 *The Case of the Deadly Ha-Ha Game*
38 *The Fling*
39 *The Secret Laundry Monster Files*
40 *The Case of the Missing Bird Dog*
41 *The Case of the Shipwrecked Tree*
42 *The Case of the Burrowing Robot*
43 *The Case of the Twisted Kitty*
44 *The Dungeon of Doom*
45 *The Case of the Falling Sky*
46 *The Case of the Tricky Trap*
47 *The Case of the Tender Cheeping Chickies*
48 *The Case of the Monkey Burglar*

49 *The Case of the Booby-Trapped Pickup*
50 *The Case of the Most Ancient Bone*
51 *The Case of the Blazing Sky*
52 *The Quest for the Great White Quail*
53 *Drover's Secret Life*
54 *The Case of the Dinosaur Birds*
55 *The Case of the Secret Weapon*
56 *The Case of the Coyote Invasion*
57 *The Disappearance of Drover*
58 *The Case of the Mysterious Voice*
59 *The Case of the Perfect Dog*
60 *The Big Question*
61 *The Case of the Prowling Bear*
62 *The Ghost of Rabbits Past*
63 *The Return of the Charlie Monsters*
64 *The Case of the Three Rings*
65 *The* Almost *Last Roundup*
66 *The Christmas Turkey Disaster*
67 *Wagons West*
68 *The Secret Pledge*

Join Hank the Cowdog's Security Force

Are you a big Hank the Cowdog fan? Then you'll want to join Hank's Security Force! Here is some of the neat stuff you will receive:

Welcome Package

- A Hank paperback
- An Original (19"x25") Hank Poster
- A Hank bookmark

Eight digital issues of *The Hank Times* with

- Lots of great games and puzzles
- Stories about Hank and his friends
- Special previews of future books
- Fun contests

More Security Force Benefits

- Special discounts on Hank books, audios, and more
- Special Members-Only section on website

Total value of the Welcome Package and *The Hank Times* is $23.99. However, your two-year membership is **only $7.99** plus $5.00 for shipping and handling.

☐ Yes I want to join Hank's Security Force. Enclosed is $12.99 ($7.99 + $5.00 for shipping and handling) for my **two-year membership**. [Make check payable to Maverick Books.]

Which book would you like to receive in your Welcome Package? (#   ) any book except #50

BOY or GIRL

YOUR NAME (CIRCLE ONE)

MAILING ADDRESS

CITY STATE ZIP

TELEPHONE BIRTH DATE

E-MAIL (required for digital Hank Times)

Send check or money order for $12.99 to:

Hank's Security Force
Maverick Books
PO Box 549
Perryton, Texas 79070

DO NOT SEND CASH. NO CREDIT CARDS ACCEPTED.

Allow 2–3 weeks for delivery.

Offer is subject to change.

The following activities are samples from *The Hank Times*, the official newspaper of Hank's Security Force. Please do not write on these pages unless this is your book. Even then, why not just find a scrap of paper?

"Photogenic" Memory Quiz

We all know that Hank has a "photogenic" memory—being aware of your surroundings is an important quality for a Head of Ranch Security. Now you can test your powers of observation.

How good is your memory? Look at the illustration on page 11 and try to remember as many things about it as possible. Then turn back to this page and see how many questions you can answer.

1. Were there clouds in the sky? Yes or No?
2. How many fence posts could you see? 1, 2, or 3?
3. Was the tail light Round, Oval, or Rectangular?
4. Was Hank looking to HIS Left or Right?
5. Could you see the pickup's license plate? Yes or No?
6. How many of Miss Beulah's eyes could you see? 1, 2, 3, or all 4?

"Word Maker"

Try making up to twenty words from the letters in the name below. Use as many letters as possible, however, don't just add an "s" to a word you've already listed in order to have it count as another. Try to make up entirely new words for each line!

Then, count the total number of letters used in all of the words you made, and see how well you did using the Security Force Rankings below!

PLATO BEULAH

59-61 You spend too much time with J.T. Cluck and the chickens.

62-64 You are showing some real Security Force potential.

65-68 You have earned a spot on our ranch security team.

69+ Wow! You rank up there as a top-of-the-line cowdog.

"Rhyme Time"

What if Hank decides he wants to leave the ranch and go in search of another job? What kind of jobs could he find?

Make a rhyme using HANK that would relate to his new job possibilities.

Example: Hank takes people to his secret spot for pond fishing.
Answer: Hank BANK

1. Hank starts a company that disposes of old boats.
2. Hank invents a new diet plan with shakes for meals.
3. Hank joins the military and becomes an officer.
4. Hank works on a pirate ship and is in charge of this.
5. Hank makes phone calls like, "Is your air conditioner running? It is. Well, you better go catch it!"
6. Hank makes a baby bedding item. (Hint: Pete helped name it.)

Answers:

1. Hank SANK
2. Hank DRANK
3. Hank RANK
4. Hank PLANK
5. Hank CRANK
6. Hankie BLANKY

Have you visited Hank's official website yet?

www.hankthecowdog.com

Don't miss out on exciting *Hank the Cowdog* games and activities, as well as up-to-date news about upcoming books in the series!

When you visit, you'll find:

- Hank's BLOG, which is updated regularly and is always the first place we announce upcoming books and new products!
- Hank's Official Shop, with tons of great Hank the Cowdog books, audiobooks, games, t-shirts, stuffed animals, mugs, bags, and more!
- Links to Hank's social media, whereby Hank sends out his "Cowdog Wisdom" to fans
- A FREE, printable Map of Hank's Ranch!
- Hank's Music Page where you can listen to songs and even download FREE ringtones!
- A way to sign up for Hank's free email updates
- Sally May's Ranch Round-up Recipes!
- Printable & Colorable Greeting Cards for Holidays
- Articles about Hank and author, John R. Erickson in the news

...AND MUCH, MUCH MORE!

search the website GO

BOOKS The Collection
FAN ZONE Fun & Games
AUTHOR Meet the Creator
STORE Books & More

HANK THE COWDOG

Find Toys, Games, Books & More at the Hank shop.

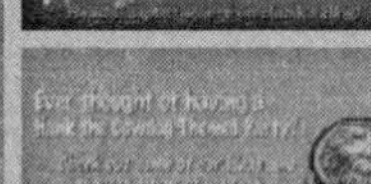

Hank Plays Cupid:

GAMES COME PLAY WITH HANK & PALS

BOOKS BROWSE THE ENTIRE HANK CATALOG

FRIENDS GET TO KNOW THE RANCH GANG

Visit Hank's Facebook page

FROM THE BLOG

JAN 26 Hank is Cupid in Disguise...

JAN 16 The Valentine's Day Robbery! - a Snippet from the Story

DEC 04 Getting SIGNED Hank the Cowdog books for Christmas!

OCT 14 Education Association's lists of recommended books?

Follow Hank on Twitter

Watch Hank on YouTube

Hank's Music.
Free ringtones, music and more!
MORE

Follow Hank on Pinterest

Send Hank an Email

VISIT THE BLOG

Official Shop
Find books, audio, toys and more!
LET'S GO

Hank's Survey
We'd love to know what you think!

GO

Get the Latest
Keep up with Hank's news and promotions by signing up for our e-news.
Looking for The Hank Times fan club newsletter?

Enter your email address
SIGN UP

TEACHER'S CORNER
Download fun activity guides, discussion questions and more.

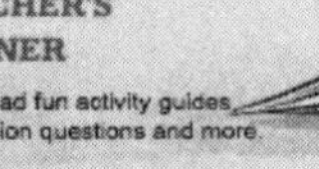

Join Hank's Security Force
Get the activity letter and other cool stuff.
JOIN

SALLY MAY'S RECIPES

Discover delicious recipes from Sally May herself.

GO

Hank in the News

Find out what the media is saying about Hank.

GO

FEATURED BOOK

The Christmas Turkey Disaster

Now Available!

Hank is in real trouble this time. L...

BUY READ LISTEN

HANK

BOOKS Browse Titles
FAN ZONE Games
AUTHOR John Erickson's Bio
SHOP The Books

And, be sure to check out the Audiobooks!

If you've never heard a *Hank the Cowdog* audiobook, you're missing out on a lot of fun! Each Hank book has also been recorded as an unabridged audiobook for the whole family to enjoy!

Praise for the Hank Audiobooks:

"It's about time the Lone Star State stopped hogging Hank the Cowdog, the hilarious adventure series about a crime solving ranch dog. Ostensibly for children, the audio renditions by author John R. Erickson are sure to build a cult following among adults as well." — *Parade Magazine*

"Full of regional humor . . . vocals are suitably poignant and ridiculous. A wonderful yarn." — *Booklist*

"For the detectin' and protectin' exploits of the canine Mike Hammer, hang Hank's name right up there with those of other anthropomorphic greats...But there's no sentimentality in Hank: he's just plain more rip-roaring fun than the others. Hank's misadventures as head of ranch security on a spread somewhere in the Texas Panhandle are marvelous situation comedy." — *School Library Journal*

"Knee-slapping funny and gets kids reading."

— *Fort Worth Star Telegram*

Love Hank's Hilarious Songs?

Hank the Cowdog's "Greatest Hits" albums bring together the music from the unabridged audiobooks you know and love! These wonderful collections of hilarious (and sometimes touching) songs are unmatched. Where else can you learn about coyote philosophy, buzzard lore, why your dog is protecting an old corncob, how bugs compare to hot dog buns, and much more!

And, be sure to visit Hank's "Music Page" on the official website to listen to some of the songs and download FREE Hank the Cowdog ringtones!

"Audio-Only" Stories

Ever wondered what those "Audio-Only" Stories in Hank's Official Store are all about? The Audio-Only Stories are *Hank the Cowdog* adventures that have never been released as books. They are about half the length of a typical *Hank* book, and there are currently seven of them. They have run as serial stories in newspapers for years and are now available as audiobooks!

Teacher's Corner

Know a teacher who uses Hank in their classroom? You'll want to be sure they know about Hank's "Teacher's Corner"! Just click on the link on the homepage, and you'll find free teachers' aids, such as a printable map of Hank's ranch, a reading log, coloring pages, blog posts specifically for teachers and librarians, and much more!

Photo Courtesy of Western Horseman Magazine

John R. Erickson, a former cowboy, has written numerous books for both children and adults and is best known for his acclaimed *Hank the Cowdog* series. The *Hank* series began as a self-publishing venture in Erickson's garage in 1982 and has endured to become one of the nation's most popular series for children and families. Through the eyes of Hank the Cowdog, a smelly, smart-aleck Head of Ranch Security, Erickson gives readers a glimpse into daily life on a cattle ranch in the West Texas Panhandle. His stories have won a number of awards, including the Audie, Oppenheimer, Wrangler, and Lamplighter Awards, and have been translated into Spanish, Danish, Farsi, and Chinese. USA Today calls the *Hank the Cowdog* books "the best family entertainment in years." Erickson lives and works on his ranch in Perryton, Texas, with his family.

Gerald L. Holmes is a largely self-taught artist who grew up on a ranch in the Oklahoma Panhandle. He has illustrated the *Hank the Cowdog* books and serial stories, in addition to numerous other cartoons and textbooks, for over thirty years, and his paintings have been featured in various galleries across the United States. He and his wife live in Perryton, Texas, where they raised their family, and where he continues to paint his wonderfully funny and accurate portrayals of modern American ranch life to this day.

Shawn Tevis Photography